The Love Letters of St. Francis and St. Clare of Assisi

The Love Letters of St. Francis and St. Clare of Assisi

The Journey of Two Great Saints, Soaked in Love, Who Changed The World

BRUCE DAVIS

Waterside Productions

Printed in the United States of America

First Printing, 2020

ISBN-13: 978-1-939116-29-1 print edition
ISBN-13: 978-1-939116-31-4 ebook edition

Waterside Productions

2055 Oxford Ave
Cardiff, CA 92007
www.waterside.com

Introduction

On September 26, 1997, there was a massive earthquake that shook Assisi, Italy, the hometown of St. Francis and St. Clare and much of neighboring Umbria. Ten people were killed, including several friars, as a large portion of the ceiling of the famous Basilica of St. Francis came crashing to the ground. Many of the ancient monasteries and churches in town suffered cracked walls or structural collapse as many quakes continued to rattle the stone buildings in the days and weeks to follow.

I was in Assisi during this time. As is often the case, we had a group of pilgrims who were looking for a sincere spiritual life while exploring the footsteps of St. Francis and St. Clare from long ago. The town leaders closed the medieval gates in the city walls. All tourists were asked to leave because of safety reasons. For some reason, our group was allowed to stay. We met each day in a hotel room at the top of town and visited the ancient churches and monasteries. They were all closed because of the earthquakes. But we would visit them nevertheless and sit outside contemplating what was happening in the town of St. Francis and St. Clare.

A few years later, I was told a good friend of mine, Brother Gerardo from San Damiano, was in a hospital for Franciscan brothers in the town below Assisi, Santa Maria della Angeli. He was dying of cancer and I wanted to be sure to see him before he died. I found the hospital next to the large church built over and around the original church of St. Francis. My friend was very ill. The room he was in was located in a long corridor of single rooms. The hallway was dark and gloomy. His room had one window, a chair, a small closet, a cross on the wall and nothing else. Not a plant, no color, nothing, he was just laying there preparing for death.

When I entered the room he lit up. I assumed he'd had few visitors and was just left there, to meditate on Sister Death, as Franciscans would call our final chapter. My friend said he had been praying I would come visit. Before I could respond, he began to tell me a remarkable story. It seemed after the earthquake several walls at San Damiano, the ancient home of St. Clare, now the home of Franciscan brothers, had fallen into much disrepair. San Damiano was set to be rebuilt as they tried to preserve the ancient walls while new ones were being erected. My friend Brother Gerardo told me that one night during this time he was sitting in the historical dormitory of St. Clare when he noticed a large crack in the wall. He went over to investigate and realized that several stones were now completely loose. He pulled out one of the stones and there was a box. It was sealed in some sort of wax.

He took the box back to his room and quietly opened it, and there was a pile of letters. He quickly realized the letters were from Francis to Clare and from Clare back to Francis. I asked him, how did Clare get back the letters she had sent Francis? He responded that he didn't really know. But he surmised that after Francis died, Clare continue to live for many years. Probably one of the brothers had found these letters from Clare to Francis and decided to return them to Clare to cheer her up. She missed Francis terribly!

Brother Gerardo told me to go to his closet and look underneath the clothes at the bottom, and the box would be there. He told me that he wanted me to have these letters. He didn't know who else to give them to. "If I gave them to someone in the Church," he explained, "they would find the letters too radical as they found Francis and Clare many years ago. The letters would probably be investigated and then buried in some church library or museum. If I gave them to someone in the press, the secular world would write about them for a few days and then they would be forgotten." He said he knew I had been bringing groups to Assisi for many years, looking for the heart of Francis and Clare in hope of finding something about our own heart. He knew I had written some books about St. Francis and spirituality which had been translated into different languages. "You are the only person I know," he explained, "that can take these letters and give them to the world."

As I held the box, he said one more thing. "Francis and Clare brought a revolution to the Church. These letters could bring a new revolution to the Church. The Church then and now are buried in scandal and doctrine. The heart, the real path to God, has been forgotten. These letters can remind everyone of the heart which is our door to the Divine."

And then he grew tired, wished me well, and said he wanted to rest. I found out he had died a couple of days later. I also learned that even though his final weeks in that lonely corridor seemed cold and uncaring to me, there is a secret, ancient ritual the brothers perform when another brother has died. And indeed Brother Gerardo was appreciated, prayed for, and loved after his departing.

The following are the letters of St. Francis and St. Clare. Indeed, they do call us all back to our hearts to discover the path to God. Whether this calling will be heard is up to each of us. I am committed to fulfilling Brother Gerardo's wish to give these letters to the world as best I can.

A Love Letter from Clare to Francis

Dear Francis,

*W*ords are never large enough or small enough to write to you but I try again. Buona sera, good evening. I always think about you at this time of sunset. It is during this hour that I put aside everything about the day which is not important and hold to my heart our inner path, the love we know. It is a good practice. I can safely say that my small light in the garden of my heart has become a diamond. I feel quite strong and God shines very bright. In a few hours in the dark of night, I will be sinking inside to our Lord in gratitude. Then I go to sleep. Thank you, Francis, for leading me on this path of chasing God, instead of worldly things. Thank you for showing me it is not really a chase at all, but rather a great finding, finding God always very close at hand, as close as my heart.

Francis, we share the true relationship. Many couples live together under one roof and never share what we know together. Certainly, I miss sometimes not having more time with you in the small moments of life. Then I think of most couples living with one another day after day, but so separate from each other in their thoughts and feelings. Francis, we have fallen in love, again and again landing in the great heart, the garden that extends forever. The eternity we know is the true poetry of life. The canticle you share is music for the heart inside every heart.

And you, Francis, how are you? You are a big fire on the mountaintop that many come to see. I wonder sometimes if they really know who they are visiting. I am sorry the Church confuses people by saying

1

you are great because you have suffered greatly. You and I both know human suffering gives nothing but perhaps a small push further into our heart, to rest on the lap of God. The empty times in life are small gifts we enjoy, to be alone with the quiet, with God. We enjoy these times living in the sweetness of God's mystery. Our path is nothing more or less then receiving. Every day is the simple peace. You in the cave of your heart, me with my budding roses, life is precious. Simple peace, and our hearts wrestle with the Divine being so much for our simple human heart. The birds, animals, planets and stars are family in these moments. Francis, I know you have tried again and again to explain to the bishops that they are no more special than our homeless friends, the lepers. The rich are no more rich than the very poor. Life's treasure is within us. Why don't people understand that everything is given in the silence of our heart?

Francis I want to tell you about a daydream I have been carrying all week. I see all the priests and ministers finally agreeing there is not so much to say! Every church large and small is just a house for God. People come and sit in silence. If we sit still, God is so present. In the silence is all and everything, so much peace. This is enough. And after sitting for a while, everyone absorbing the goldenness of God in our hearts, the people share bread. The church should be a place to share simple peace, food, and herbs for healing. There is so much need. This is the real church! Why do they make it so complicated Francis? Why?

Anyway this is not the reason I write. I write today trying to put some words to where I have been led inside. I know you already know. But maybe my words support you as well. I know you are burning inside in this fire. Love lightens and overwhelms all my human edges. This very, very, very bright light rises from deep inside of me. I just pray to be available. Truly God knows we are only human. My selfishness is just part of my humanness. This is not to make excuses; but Francis we really should not punish ourselves for being human. We are what we are. Can I say that in truth we are this light, only this light? When we leave this world and all our limitations, the angels will welcome us and we will know for certain. There is so much light!

Francis, I know some of the brothers are praying that your tears will stop for the sake of your health. But Francis, don't stop. I understand why you cry and cry so much. It is because of this light. Your tears are the blood of your soul and my soul as well. You cry for all of us. I pray you never stop crying. Know that each tear is milk and honey for my soul and the soul in everyone. May your joy cry out to all now and forever! In the great silence, only joy, joy, joy! I know it doesn't need to be said but thank you Francis. Thank you!

Yours, forever in our Lord,

Clare

Lady Poverty Visits the Vatican:

Letter from Francis to Clare

Dear Clare,

I hope I am not intruding upon your silence.

Thank you for your recent letter. To have your heart so close is a blessing with no beginning or ending. Yes, there is much light and tears. It is amazing how much of the Divine our small human heart can feel. All I can do is keep a small nest in my heart for the Divine to come visit and rest as She wishes. This is enough.

Recently, I was walking through the villages and heard so many people talking about the new coming of our Lord. Don't they know He is already here? Don't they realize he is no further than our hearts? I don't understand why the Church gives voice to these rumors. The longing the people have could be satisfied so quickly if they turned it inside, if they let go and fell into the arms of our Lord within.

Yesterday, I was resting on a nearby mountaintop and I had this dream. Lady Poverty was visiting Mother Church in Rome. In the dream She is approaching the palace with its high marble walls. She is knocking at the front door. The guards come and push her away. She returns and continues knocking. Three men arrive in long colorful robes, each wearing large crosses with jewels. They open the door, look everywhere, but do not see Her. A priest comes and says She must have an appointment.

She continues knocking. She knocks and knocks into the night. Finally, the bishop of Rome hears Her and comes to the door. It is now late and he is in his nightclothes. He invites Her in. In a small pantry nearby, he serves Her tea and cookies. They have so much fun and lots of humor together. The bishop begins to ask Lady Poverty, "How do I tell the rich that it is not a matter of becoming poor but..." In that moment She interrupts him. She reaches across the table and takes hold of both of his hands. There is a big smile in Her heart. Tears form in his eyes. Finally She says, "You really should try to warm this place up." They embrace one another and She suddenly disappears into the night.

Yes, Clare, we must warm this place up! There is so little love. Where is the joy? Nothing else is important! I try to tell my brothers. "Don't be distracted. Don't be so busy. Why worry about tomorrow when today there are so many gifts to open?" I know, Clare, you are reminding the sisters the same. I hear you telling them, "Our Lord is here! Come join me in the garden. In the stillness, inside the Rose of our heart, Heaven is burning, bursting in joy!"

Many of the simple people understand but many, especially the rich and powerful, they always want more. There is never enough. How do we tell them that the real riches are inside? May we all come to the peaceful heart. Surely then peace will guide us all to the living Church.

Clare, Lady Poverty has found a home in your simplicity. May you be held and protected in your golden silence. May your meditation touch the world. Mother Church needs you! Someday, you and your sisters will stand in front of the Church, offering life's true Bread to many. Angels will dance. Smiles will replace hardened faces. Gardens of the heart will grow everywhere.

Thank you for being your light, you're All.

Thank you for being my true friend and lover of God.

Truly yours,

Francis

Simple Peace:
Letter from Clare to Francis

My dear Francis,

Francis, I know there is only one reason to be truly excited and this is when our Lord visits us in our hearts. But regarding Earthly news, I must tell you while many worry about wars and lack of food in the coming winter, my sisters are singing and bathing daily in the light within their hearts. I too had a dream. Someday Kings and Queens, the rich and powerful, people from all over the world, will be coming to Assisi not to judge you but to ask how they can join you on your path. What will you tell them? Will you ask them to throw their riches into the river? Will you tell them to give all their power away? Francis, are you ready for the world to be at your feet like the little birds in your garden? Imagine everyone with one prayer, one heart, asking "Lord make me an instrument!"

Peace, Francis, peace—this is what you should teach! Let them keep their possessions. Let them keep their worldly power. Share with them the simple peace. This is enough. Tell them about the beauty of peace in every moment. Give them the simple steps that you and I know so well. Step by step, peace and more peace with everyone and everything. This will be a good beginning. Once they feel the peace, what do riches and power have to offer? Why would they chase after earthly comforts when they have life's true treasure? Once they feel the peace inside what else is of value but wanting to serve one another?

Everyone wants peace, Francis, but they do not know the source of this peace. You must teach them. Real peace comes only from a peaceful heart! And a peaceful heart comes from finding so much God inside that there is no room for anything else but peace.

When the princes and princesses of the world come to Assisi, take them on top of Mt. Subasio. Ask them to be quiet and listen to Sister Wind. Invite them to let Brother Silence carve out a home in the stillness of their heart. "Here is peace. Prayer is the simplicity of your own heart." Francis, I hear your words. "All we need to do is offer everything in our heart." Sit with them Francis. Tell them not to be in such a hurry! Ask them to sit and feel our Lord's presence. Let them know, "There is an inner garden!" Teach them Francis that peace is a practice. Every day we go to the sacred well of peace inside our hearts. As peace becomes more important, our self-importance becomes less. Slowly, slowly we become instruments with a sound that is beautiful and true. Peace is not something that happens in the world. Peace happens in our world as we make friends with the nakedness of our heart. Francis, this is your teaching, your life. It is no accident so many brothers have come to you from so many corners of Italy and neighboring countries. You have shown us all, God is no further away than our heart.

Francis, I remember our time together recently in the olive trees at San Damiano. We talked all day without a word spoken. In the perfect silence, we shared everything in our hearts. The birds, little flowers, trees, the whole world seemed in complete agreement. Then the farmers from nearby came running up to us saying they saw flames and smoke! It was only you and me Francis, sitting, looking at one another, burning inside in simple peace.

I never shared with you, Francis, but that night I cried myself to sleep. There were so many tears of gratitude for all the milk and honey God has opened in my heart. The tears would not stop; neither does my gratitude for what we give to one another.

Thank you Francis, eternally thank you.

Yours truly in our Lord.

Always,
Clare

New Beginning for Mother Church:
Letter from Francis to Clare

Dear Clare,

Thank you for your recent letter. Thank you for sharing the simple peace. In morning light, little flowers are opening and spreading color and peace everywhere. Yes, simple peace for us all!

Recently some of the brothers have come to me insisting that I make a rule for all the brothers. What should they carry on their journey? What possessions should they keep in their small hut? One brother asks if he can have a walking stick. I say no if this stick means he will lean on it instead of leaning on God inside of him. Why would he want to carry a walking stick when carrying God in our heart is more than enough? Another brother asks if he can keep his books. I ask him why would he want a busy mind full of all kinds of things when we could enjoy a calm, peaceful heart full of God?

But Clare to be honest, these problems are the small things to be concerned with. What do I tell the brother who is possessed with pride? He gave up his worldly possessions and now thinks he is so special. There is the brother who is constantly busy cleaning and organizing his little hut and surrounding huts as if God will only come and visit if everything is in perfect order. And there is the brother who is always trying to tell others what to do. He thinks he is God's general, but as far as I know,

God has no need for soldiers, no less generals. There is the brother who gets angry over small things not going his way. Many of the brothers find need for comfort when in fact they already have everything they could possibly want. Then all the brothers, myself included, are way too serious too much of the time. Where is our joy? How do I tell the brothers to give these possessions away? These are the things which can stick to a soul, leaving God little room to surface in our heart. If our heart is possessed by so much self where is there room for love?

Clare, I was recently sitting on top of Mt. Subasio in the darkness of night. While waiting slowly for first morning light, I was looking over the valley below. My brothers were sleeping soundly in their camp not too far below. I asked the angels to sit next to each brother as he opened his eyes and took a first breath of the new day. Suddenly I understood! If I practice a little compassion for the brother who wants his walking stick, maybe he will find some generosity and share his stick with another brother who is not feeling well. And the brother who is feeling ill, maybe he will find some lightness in his heart and hug the brother who is always cleaning, organizing, and tell him he is loved exactly as he is. Then this brother, instead of being busy, will feel his innocence. He could sit with our soldier brother and tell him the war is over. No more orders, peace is here!

Clare, instead of the brothers working so hard to give up their possessions, maybe they can enjoy what they have! If one brother finds simplicity, surely he will be an example of simplicity for those around him. When another brother finds forgiveness, surely his love will teach the others to embrace more and complain less. One humble brother could touch many of us who are filled with self-importance. Another brother who surrenders to his heart could teach all of us about trust. Then there is Brother Silence, who in his sweet quiet is reminding us all that instead of being occupied with words, a great light is waiting inside of us. There is the brother who first thing every morning goes and collects bread for the lepers living nearby. He is teaching us about dignity, honor, and life's purpose. The smiles on the faces of the lepers eating well at the beginning of the day is God's beauty and goodness for all of us to see.

You see, Clare, maybe no rule is possible. Maybe no rule is necessary! For God to exist, love must be present. And when love is present, the heart blossoms into a garden that speaks for itself. I am the first to confess I must tell my brothers less what to do and more how beautiful they are.

Love is God's perfect instrument. Meanwhile, Clare, you and me in our small little way, we just are what we are. Truly, God knows everything in our heart. Instead of being so focused on what we should not have and not be doing, maybe we should just focus on the joy. Every moment, every day is so much joy, so much God.

Clare, it has been a long winter and late spring. Many of the brothers are tied in the knot of self- doubt and struggle. They worry too much. They judge themselves, our path, and one another. Why do we judge so much instead of feeling the peace that is completely present? We all stay busy with things to do instead of being simply happy. There is a happy room within which no bad weather can take away. I know now I can help my brothers throw these possessions into the melting snow. I will breathe my joy into their heart!

Pray for me, Clare. Pray. May our joy help all our brothers and sisters throw everything into the river until there is only light, immense light flowing fast and free from our heart out everywhere in the world!

I wish you only peace, the true peace of our Lord in your innermost garden.

Yours truly,
Francis

Come Down off the Mountain: Letter from Clare to Francis

Dear Francis,

Thank you for your letter. Yes, breathe your big joy into the heart of each and every brother. May they be so full of our Lord that life's small difficulties grow even smaller. May we all feel your courage and truth in our every step.

Today I feel moved to write you. I know you enjoy spending your days on the mountaintops where it is only you, your friends the little creatures, and Sister Wind carrying your soul to sacred realms. But we need you. The people need you. We need your words, which fly directly from your heart to the heart in all of us. Ordinary words from the minds of men have difficulty reaching the heart. But your words are flowers and stones, rain and sunshine of only truth. There is no possibility to judge or find some way to push them away. Francis, we need you to come down off the mountain and support us all to unlock God's love hidden within us.

When the local priests talk about God or holiness the people yawn and close their ears. The people listen and quickly put the words into their pocket and continue their day. But God, holiness, these words are the proven way, feeding the hungry little bird of every soul. Francis when you use these words it is like a sharp arrow that breaks through everyone's self-importance and cuts into the soul where the real treasure is found. The heart's full path is too precious for defensiveness, judgments about Mother Church, and all the excuses we have not to pursue the Golden Realms. When you say the word holiness everyone sees your open arms. Holiness pours out of your nakedness and washes our heart. We need you Francis to tell the secrets you find on the mountaintop. Tell us about holiness which comes out of a great humility of seeing how human we are. Speak to us about holiness, the small light deep in the heart. When we give, offer ourselves to this small light, holiness grows. It is as if emerging out of a dark cave. The light, God's light expands and expands inside of us. It is an immense light going forever!

Francis, please come down from the mountain and speak to us, my sisters included. Tell us about your gentle inner life in the silence. This is what will bring the people back to Church and God. Your presence of heart reminds all of us there is so much more than our thoughts. Francis, when you climb the mountain, you leave everything behind, you give God your all and everything. This unleashes the fire that burns inside of you. We need your fire to burn in us as well. When you speak, we feel the difference between thinking about God, believing in God, and knowing God. Your words take us to the pure light deep inside where only God, so much God is present. You bring us to the place within where there is only peace, endless peace. In your words, our longing is heard. Francis you understand.

I guess you are wondering why I am so excited today as I beg you to come off the mountain and visit us. To be honest, as I sit in our little cloister garden the little flowers have opened in my heart to a vast valley of flowers. There is so much peace. I offer the peace to you, everyone, and everything. There is more and even more peace expanding forever. Francis when you speak, you speak for my heart. This is why I write. Please come down off the mountain and help rebuild a fallen church!

Today I am drowning in the peace of the little flowers and your big fire lights the world, my world. I hope you do not find my request too selfish. I am your sister and friend in the simple footsteps, each joyful step, stone by stone. We find one another in the depths of our soul, in God. There is so much!

Thank you, dear Francis. Thank you from the sweetest flowers of my innermost garden.

Yours always in our Lord,

Clare

What Could I Say?:
Letter from Francis to Clare

Dear Clare,

Your thirst for the living God touches me deeply. Yes, God must be alive to move in people's hearts. Otherwise the words have no fire, no water, no breath for life and joy. But dear Clare, have no worry. God's plan is much more than anything we could imagine no less make by our own effort. If we are simple little flowers giving our all the best we can, this is enough!

As more and more people discover the richness of the heart, surely they will want to serve the poor and share their treasure. What would the world would be like if everyone was first of the heart and then of the mind? What if people from all walks of life awakened and wanted nothing less then to give themselves in service to the poor, lonely, and the ill? Imagine instead of being busy with the endless details of daily life, buying things we really do not need, we all found our purpose of being present with God's presence in this moment. Imagine love being poured out into the streets. People everywhere could be in search for our Lord in the faces of their neighbors, the plants, the animals, and the stars.

Imagine us all joining you in a search for the true love instead of spending so much time being comfortable in their position and home. If we have a little humility, do you think it could flow down into the small huts and grand castles around the world like a gentle stream of warm love?

I promised always to be frank with you. So many are lost it is a wonder that any of us can be found. We must ask ourselves what is necessary for a true life? How do we know if we are feeling the flames for God or just some passion of the day? How do we know if we are sharing the real soothing water for all who thirst? Is walking the path with no possessions but having our naked heart the answer? We know there are no big plans or special knowledge that will rebuild a fallen church. Is the gifts of the moment, the compassion, gentleness, devotion, and of course our simplicity, the answer for all the brothers and sisters coming to join us?

I try to tell each new brother that we must love where there is no love, cry where there are no tears, and laugh where there is no laughter. Our Lord is much more than the Lord of the Cross. He is the Lord of every human heart waiting to be appreciated and received.

Clare, you and I both know that the Church is not something to build but a love story to include our little friends, the creatures, believers and non- believers, a love story for everyone and everything including the planets and the stars.

Yes, I was asked to come down from the mountain and tell what I know. But what do I know? I am just a small worm in God's great garden. Sister Wind sings to the creatures surrounding my small grotto. Brother Sun warms us even in winter so we can stay in gratitude for the life which is given. And every night the stars take my soul on a journey. There are no words. But I know you know that our small human heart can stretch out to the farthest stars in the sky. God is so large inside of us and yet we are so human, quick to disappointment and selfish wants. What can I tell the people down the mountain? How small I am and how great our Lord? I am sure he already knows this. My tears are just a few drops in the great seas of love and pain felt by everyone.

Forgive me Clare, but I have nothing to say. Silence has grabbed my being and poured its substance over every inch of every thought and every feeling. I can only worship, forgive, and praise what the silence reveals to me. I can only reach as deep inside as I can and receive the heart of the silence that is beating so softly, lovingly, offering to carry me to heights I cannot find words for.

I am forever yours, in the heart which is the heart of God in each of us.

Your,

Francis

Scandal:
Letter from Clare to Francis

Dear Francis,

Your words have the sound of eternity and I feel compelled to write about scandal and mistrust which has come to our door. And do I dare say to the door of your brothers!

Forgive me Francis for what I am about to say. Everyone in Assisi knows there is a convent in the lower part of town that has a special drawer that is approached in the alley and opened inside the walls of the monastery. Normally, the sons and daughters of the wealthy leave unwanted newly born babies in this drawer. On the other side of the wall, the sisters inside come and take care. They find parents for the poor little ones left so alone.

Francis, listen closely. One of my dear sisters is with child and she threatens to leave her baby in that drawer! What's more, she says the father is one of your brothers whom she will not name. They both are afraid and ashamed!

I don't know which brother. They all are human. We are all so very human. I think it is the brother who leaves fresh eggs once or twice a week. Or it could be the new brother from down south who at sunset often comes to sing and serenade the sisters about the new moon and all the beauty in nature. Does it matter who the father is? Does any of this matter in the eyes of our Lord?

Francis, I thought we are all here just to pray for our souls and praise God. Why does earthly life sneak so deeply into our convent walls? Who am I to judge this sister? Who am I to seek out the father? Are not desires of the flesh as natural as flowers growing in the garden, birds making nests, and children laughing in the fields? Francis why is the silence of my heart interrupted with these matters? You and I have our own emotions that play with our mind and heart. Each day we decide which life we want to live, a life of householder or brother and sister. Each day we try to keep our gaze fixed, our concentration true to the brightest light, the light streaming from deep inside of us.

For this light, we give up everything. We leave our family, our worldly desires, our belongings, our self. This light is so true, so complete in love that in truth you and I know Francis, we give up nothing. This light is our all and everything.

Now one of my sisters and one of your brothers is hiding from everyone. What's worse, they are hiding from themselves the beauty of a newborn child that soon will be here in the world. Surely they cannot just slip away in the night and abandon the baby in the box in the convent's wall! Surely they know this is the Christ Child they are carrying. Every baby is the Christ child waiting for our love. Francis, don't think me mad. I know it is almost July but my thoughts are with Christmas. A child is to be born!

What do we do with everyone's judgments? What do we do with the Lord who is going to be born and born soon to a quiet, young sister without a roof of her own?

Pray for us Francis. Fortunately every child no matter how small and how alone has the soul of a full-grown adult, a guardian angel, and is cared for by God. I tell the sister to remember this. A path will be found for this new family, a path of humility and joy!

May all the angels be with this child and all children who come into this world! May the angels be with each of us as we stand in the light of what is right and what is true.

Francis, maybe this shadow passes through the convent to remind us of the light. Maybe the light will even be brighter as we remember why we chose this life. Each day we must remember why we sing each morning with all our heart. We must remember to receive the finish of evening with prayer, sitting together in a long moment of peace. I cherish this peace.

Yours in light,

Clare

God, Only God: Letter from Francis to Clare

Dear Clare,

I understand your concern about your dear little sister and the baby that is in her womb. The Lord watches over all of us, especially the little ones. We must not forget this but be always mindful and heart full of the needs of others because if we don't offer our hands to help who can the lord call upon?

I write today because maybe my experience will shine light on this small shadow that is passing over our community. There is so much God. He is the smell of the pine trees this time of year in the forest. He is the hawk and small birds as they scramble each day to find the little shrubs which satisfy their bellies. He is the dancing clouds which come out of nowhere and in a few minutes disappear into air. I am often full of gratitude I saw them the few brief moments they were here.

There is so much God. He is in the small plate of berries that a dear brother brings to me after morning prayer. He is the brother smiling at me, proud that we are friends. There is so much God. He is the emptiness in my heart which fills for no reason at all minutes later in a peace which is otherworldly. I don't know how to explain where or how this peace comes. But I know it is Him! He is my impatience, my selfishness, in each of my aches and pains as they roll through my body from limb to limb day after day. It's all God. The pain, the joy, the beauty, all God.

So when a shadow passes over our community or over our own hearts we should not be overly concerned. It too is God, we just don't see this in the moment. If we practice our concentration of heart, keep the light in what we see, hear, think, and do, there will be only more God.

Yesterday I was given some food from a beggar who didn't like what was on his plate. He wanted to test me to see if I would eat the leftovers from the leftovers he could not eat. At first I looked at this food and it looked terrible. Then I looked again and it was a fresh garden salad from your garden. Instead of this angry man insisting I eat his food, it was you Clare serving me God, everything fresh and beautiful right from the garden of your heart. I do not know how to explain it. It was love, that is all I can say. It was love.

Thank you Clare for loving me so I can love. Thank you for the honesty of your soul so I can be honest. Thank you for being so I can truly be.

In the name of love and everything good we cast out the shadows that appear in life.

We cast them out! Love, Clare, only love. God, Clare and more God.

Yours,

Francis

Our African Brother:
Letter from Francis to Clare

My dear Clare,

Your recent note is so deep in my heart, I must, yes I must, write you again. The shadow over this world is also over our brothers and our sisters. All we can do is keep our hearts in the light. This light grows in our understanding. This light shines in our giving. This light is pure and true in each of us. We can trust this light and live in this light in certainty.

I, too, have news of shame and disrespect from my community. There is a new brother, a big brother with an even bigger heart and smile! He is from Africa. He was a street child with no home. The Church cared for him. As he grew older, he grew in the Church, now coming to Assisi to be a wonderful brother. We are very fortunate to have him. His heart is a big hug from God for everyone who knows him.

So how do my brothers treat him? I am ashamed to say this but they call him "monkey." They make him eat alone or sit with other brothers from foreign lands. These brothers, who say they are brothers of mine, wear a brown robe with a rope tied around their waists. I can't believe they call themselves brothers. I cried when I heard this news. I cried!

I have heard my African friend has returned to his land, his people. The Church there is jealous of his big heart and popularity with his people. The Church has placed many constraints upon him. He has left the Church and the brothers. He has taken off his robe and the rope around his waist and is now selling blankets to help feed his neighbors. Shame, Clare, shame for all of us.

I have to admit, these stories about my brothers disturb me deeply. I know these brothers. They are good people who are also very wrong. They are like the disciples who betrayed our Lord. My African brother, the brothers from foreign lands are no threat to the others. They come not to take but to be part of our great outpouring of joy. There is no competition. The Lord provides enough food for each of us. We have even more when we share with those in our midst who have nothing but a smile just to have something to eat. Despite good intentions, many brothers are crippled with ideas from their past. But this is no excuse. We are brothers!

I thought, if my brothers gave up their worldly possessions, their worldly lives, they would find so much God that only love would be present. I was wrong. Instead they argue about what it means to give up our possessions. They argue about what it means to leave the world. They debate instead of love.

How can I stay on the mountaintop in prayer when there is so much injustice below? Clare, please tell me if I am wrong, but I feel there are many seasons. There is a season to be in the towns and villages living with the poor and letting them know they are not alone. And there is a season for me to be alone, just me and my Lord on the mountaintop. I need help with all my nakedness and only God can clothe me in some truth.

We are here to guide one another to the light. It is this great light that is our source, our strength, our purpose. In this light we find no greater desire but to share what we have with others who have less. With our Lord's grace, may we become instruments of this light. Clare may you rest in this light and may it brighten every moment of your day.

Yours truly,

Francis

$\mathcal{A}$ $\mathcal{L}ong$ $\mathcal{W}alk$:
$\mathcal{L}etter$ $from$ $\mathcal{C}lare$ to $\mathcal{F}rancis$

My dear Francis,

It is Sunday morning. After Morning Prayer and sitting for a long time in the sweetness of our chapel, all the sisters went for a long walk. I asked the oldest sister who walks the slowest to lead us. She wove us through the olive trees up in the woods near Assisi. She took us far enough up the mountain where we could have a good view of the entire valley and yes, a view of the valley in this moment of our lives.

In the beginning I was thinking about all that has to be done. There are so many details to the kitchen and, of course, in my garden always so much to do. Slowly, slowly I began to enjoy the walk. When we came to a large stone sitting next to the path, my thoughts went to you and the brothers. I know the Lord is in your midst. But how can your simple and humble gathering move the big stone of all the troubles in Mother Church? How is such a thing possible? Then immediately I remembered that the stone at the grave of our Lord mysteriously moved. He has risen! With this thought, finally my mind stopped. One thought remembering our Lord; finally, I felt my heart again. I don't know what people do who don't remember. Do they live in their thoughts all the time without any peace?

Anyway, at the end of the walk which was all in silence, all the sisters sat together under the olive trees next to the convent. We sat for a long time just being together without words. Then one of our sisters, the youngest, who just joined us from Naples, began to sing. Her voice was a gentle offering, "Lord you are my heart, my all, my everything" over and over again. Her soul was a shower of warm wind full of flower petals landing all around and over us. I felt you with us, Francis, in that moment. I often feel you with me in moments like these. Afterward, we sat listening to the olive trees, the little flowers, and Sister Wind. There was so much presence everywhere. For many minutes, I loved looking around at all the sisters. Their eyes were closed in peace. I noticed that our pregnant sister was holding her belly. She has a new smile in her heart.

Another sister began talking and shared how in the beginning of the walk she could think of only her physical pains and challenges just to be with us for the journey. But after a while, she began counting God's presence in all the different shades of the color green she could find. She found twenty-six shades of green. She was very proud of herself. So much God! More sisters shared. It was good to take a walk to nowhere in particular, no purpose in mind, to spend the afternoon letting the silence slowly walk inside of us. Francis, for you and me, every day is Sunday. And people think our lives are so difficult. They think we suffer and give up so much. To endure this life, they think that we are special. Little do they realize we just enjoy the Sunday of life!

I had a laugh returning inside the convent, imagining you Francis, me, our communities inviting all to take Sunday walks. Francis do you think we could teach the Church to dance, laugh, and cry again? Can our Church lead us to love? Each of us is called to love as our Lord did not so long ago. I am not waiting for our Lord to return. He is here. We just have to take more walks, enjoy more silence, and be close to the heart of the slowest member of our family.

Francis, I guess you must know there are many letters that I never actually send to you. You are occupied enough emptying your own busy mind. You don't need my thoughts weighing you down. I write nevertheless. I put many of these letters in a small box under my bed. Then I know while I am sleeping, you, God, the story of our heart continue.

Be well Francis. Be very happy. May you find many, many shades of green.

Yours,
Clare

A New Brother:
Letter from Francis to Clare

Dear Clare,

A new brother arrived today. You won't believe this but he arrived on his horse in full armor, with spear, and sword at his side. He jumped off his horse and announced to me and the few brothers standing by, "I am here to report to Sir Francis! I am ready to do battle for my Lord and swear in the name of my family to give all of my being to serve and do my best." Little brother Juniper jumped back in fear. The new brother didn't know me, so he was looking for "Sir Francis" to report to. Slowly I introduced myself. I guess I was not exactly what he expected. To be honest, he was not what I expected either.

We invited him to take off his armor and have a cup of tea around the fire with us. It was a hot day, so we could only imagine how extra hot he was in his war attire. Juniper offered some water to his horse as well. "Why do you think you need to do battle for our Lord?" I asked. "Because heathens are stealing the hearts and minds of innocent souls," he quickly replied. "And what are you going to do with these heathens?" I asked. "Slay them, of course! Unless you tell me just to capture them. But what could you do with them after that? What good are they? You can't change their ways."

I took a deep breath. "You know, until recently, there were many who thought I and my brothers were heathens. I'm glad you are not here to slay us!" The new brother quickly interrupted, "Of course not, your reputation as a soldier of Christ reached our village in the north country long ago." I replied, "I am a soldier with no weapons but my heart. Are you ready to throw away all your weapons and just stand with us with your heart?"

The new brother looked at me for a while and began taking off more of his armor as Juniper and another brother began looking for a robe for him.

I began thinking of so many members of our Church. There are many Christians ready with their armor to fight the enemies of Christ. How many wars have we fought when our Lord specifically told us to turn our cheek and forgive seven times seventy anyone who has wronged us? What can we offer to all the soldiers who are ready to find wrong with anyone they disagree with? How do we explain that the real war is with the war in our hearts? Do we dare point to the ill, the children, and innocent who live in our midst needing a war of care and attention? Can we tell the soldiers in the Church to take off the armor covering their naked heart?

My new brother without his horse, sword, and spear suddenly looked very different with a robe on instead. He looked vulnerable as if asking, "What am I going to do now?" I told him, "To get started there is one prayer I want you to make morning, noon, and night. Whenever you find your thoughts wandering away from the simple peace of living here with the brothers, I want you to offer everything in your heart. Yes, offer everything, all your concerns, your doubts, your wishes, whatever you find. Offer what it is in your heart. And then when you are quiet inside, go deep in your heart and receive our Lord."

The brother looked at me as if I was a wild bear or something totally foreign. He was trying to organize in his mind what I had just said. If I had told him to guard the southern entrance to the camp or to watch over the food supplies he would have quickly understood. I will never forget the look on his face as I asked him to offer everything in his heart. Finally, I said, "Don't worry. You stay with simple brother Juniper and he will show you."

Clare, helping one brother to take off his armor and find his heart is one thing. But what can we offer to all those who want to fight instead of absorbing the love which is present? What can we offer to the armor of the rich and powerful? There is the armor of the intellectuals trying to protect the doctrine of their faith. Then there is the armor that we all carry to stop us from seeing the nakedness of our heart. Clare you and I know how vulnerable life is. How can we give, really give? Brother Death is never far away. How can we disarm enough to carry love as its only weapon?

People say the Church is strong and powerful and this is the problem. Our Lord is naked and generous. On the Cross, the soldiers tease and tempt him. He looks at his mother and tells his followers to follow her. There is not a word to his tormentors. He offers everything to God and receives God in his heart.

Can we follow in the same footsteps? Surely our concerns are not as great as our Lord on the Cross. Today this new brother is like a Roman soldier. Someday may he be on the way to being one of the disciples. I was only giving a suggestion, "Offer everything you carry in your heart. "I didn't go into the rest of our normal greeting about living with us in simplicity and compassion. We are brothers looking out for the lepers living down the road and others who come to us with nothing but a wish for something to eat.

Our Lord never said anything about building a church. He never said anything about armies defending the faith. He had no doctrine to judge others but simply said he who is without sin throw the first stone. He did not become a tax collector but just the opposite. He invited the tax collector to join him. Oh, Clare, what can I and our humble brothers do?

Peace. I hear your heart repeating to me, peace. Yes, simple peace and more gentle peace. This is the war we are waging. Against all odds, we wage peace. We must pray more. Brother humility is waging the greatest battle of all! Clare, we are of one heart, now, and in eternity.

Thank you. Your brother,

Francis

The Role of Women:
Letters from Clare to Francis

Dear Francis,

Three sisters arrived yesterday from a wealthy family in Vienna. They were tired, hungry, fearful of being followed. They were certain their father and a small army was looking for them. The oldest is only seventeen. The youngest is but a child, twelve. The father, a powerful baron in Austria, was in the midst of interviewing men to marry all the daughters. He was planning one large wedding for all his daughters upon deciding the proper suitors. The mating arrangements were the talk of the whole countryside. Money, beautiful young ladies, power are all part of the story. The daughters are not happy. They are being given a choice to follow their father's demands or leave the house for a nearby Benedictine Convent. They are told they either listen to their father or live their lives out as nuns forever apart from their friends and everything important to them. Upon getting out of their carriage the youngest ran over and held me, "I want to live with you Clare." She held me tighter, "I want to love God. I want to be free!"

The other girls defended their younger sister saying they refused to be thrown into the house of some older man. They ran away instead of being forced into a marriage they didn't want. Going into some convent and being forgotten by the world was not an option. They quickly told us of the many dangers traveling across Europe alone. They pleaded with me to let them stay and be my sisters.

Francis, as you know their story is very similar to my own. I am glad to be a refuge for women threatened with no place to go. But I am not a home for young girls with no place to go but to come to Clare. Running from tyrannical fathers is not the reason to become my sister. We are here because our hearts are called. We feel this great love inside and don't want to sacrifice this love in a loveless world. We don't want to be thrown into some convent. Women deserve a life of great heart just like you Francis, and the brothers.

We deserve a home where we can listen and follow our Lord. Isn't it time for women to have their own place in the world, in the Church of our Lord, and be heard? We are in the twelfth century, how long do women have to wait to make their own decisions? If I can lead my sisters in pursuit of the great love, don't you think all women are capable of making decisions to find their path?

Francis in all honesty, isn't it time for the Church to be talking to me and my sisters as well? Are not our hearts, our commitment, our lives worthy to be heard? Of course, I respect you Francis. You know I am forever grateful for the doorway you created for me away from my father's house. You know I appreciate you sheltering me from a life hidden behind the closed doors of some convent.

But don't you agree with me, it's time for women to have a role in determining their own life? I can't even communicate this to Mother Church. How would I get a letter out but maybe through you or some other man who has contact with the men leading the Church of Rome?

Francis, you know it was Mary, Our Holy Mother, who carried, loved the Lord, and brought Him into this world for all to adore. Today it is my heart and the hearts of all women who hold their men and hold their newborn children. Our Lord spoke often with and visited women as He continues to do so now. Our Lord pointed to His mother for the disciples to follow when He was gone. It was women who first found his tomb empty. It was women who first recognized He has risen. Women and our Lord have a bond of iron and steel. Nothing, no one, can take this bond apart.

Don't you think it is time that women everywhere are given the freedom you gave me to make their own way and find their path to the great heart of God?

Francis, today I imagine a world where women are honored and respected for the holiness that lies hidden in our breast. This holiness should not have to hide. Beautiful and holy as we are, it's time for women to be treated and loved as our Lord treated and loved us in his short life among us.

Yours truly, always,

Clare

Dear Francis,

Today three young women, girls really, arrived from Austria. They announced no obstacle, no danger, nothing would stop them from join-ing us from following their heart and being close to our Lord. We quickly welcomed them and prepared rooms for them to join the sisters. Their hearts are so young and so passionate about becoming one with Christ.

I asked if they have permission to join us from their parents but they refused to discuss the matter. "We are here," they insisted. "There is no place other for us to be. We want to be free with you and your sisters to love God, love life, and follow our Lord wherever he leads us in the great adventure."

Francis, I am blessed. Three new sisters have arrived. Each is full of the passion, commitment, and thirst to sit at our Lord's feet.

Yours,

Clare

Dear Francis,

Finally, this is my third try to write this letter. Three young ladies from Austria arrived today at our convent. They are escaping their father who is pressuring them to marry rich barons who are more than twice their age.

Their hearts are made of angels too pure for such a worldly life. Of course we welcome them. They are so happy after their hard journey to be here in the peace of our little olive grove, in the peace of our small circle of sisters.

Already they are joining us in our silence and our prayer. Someday, Francis, Mother Church must make it easier for women to find a life of heart. They should not have to run in fear from Austria all the way to Assisi to have hope and breathe free air.

Our convent is filling quickly. But to be honest, I don't know if these women are coming purely to express their love for God or arrive at our door afraid of what other life confronts them. Francis, we want sisters. But we want sisters whose heart is singing the song of joy not trying to sing simply to avoid the harshness of their parents or their new husbands. The sweetness of a woman's soul should be totally free, so this sweetness can fill the air, all the valleys, and villages with the true love. Our Holy Mother is the mother of all. And this love which is Mother deserves our worship. Our Mother holds and shelters each and every one of us. May She be close to you Francis, very close in your every vulnerability, trial, and difficulty.

I am with you.

Yours,
Clare

Recovering in the Hills of the Rieti Valley: Letter from Francis to Clare

Dear Clare,

Your letter arrives just at the right moment. I am in the hills above the vast Rieti Valley. I am recovering from pains which do not seem to cease, ills which will not go away. I surrender. With God's will, I know I am recovering. I just want to rest a while in His gentle arms. In His mercy yesterday I asked for wine. The brothers said there was none. But mysteriously as they returned with the jug of water while they were carrying it, the water had turned into wine. My body today is better with the fruit of our Lord. Each day I slowly rise and make my way to our small chapel for prayer. I empty my heart. My body is already broken and empty. My heart is but a simple nest ready for God's grace, a small ray of light. He comes. Clare, He comes! I am blessed.

Yes, I too think there must be a new Church, a new way for all. Right now all I can say is my hope that in my weakness and you in your strength together maybe we can join in a Heavenly bond. Your strength, my weakness, we will bring light into darkness, wholeness where there is only disrepair. My grotto on this hillside is only a day's donkey ride from the towers of Rome. But inside I am alone. There are only me and my Lord slowly climbing the mountain, the holy mountain. I must climb. Soon I will feel better and the climb will be easier.

Clare, be the diamond that you really are. Be so clear, so pure, so true. May your new young sisters realize they have more than escaped worldly life, they have found the great treasure.

May there be only goodness for each of you. The Lord is truly with you in your little grove of olive trees. Surely, there will be a new role for women in his Church. There must! Your love is nothing less than spring for every living soul, spring for all life. The world needs, I need this spring which is you Clare. Fly with the spring dancing in your heart, fly for the whole world. Someday we both will take wing together. Someday...

Truly Yours,

Francis

Words:
Letter from Clare to Francis

Dear Francis,

These words that we share are God in flesh. Love is God in flesh. Every time you open your heart and your words pour forth, I feel like I am coming home. To have a home and someone to share this home with, this is so beautiful, such a blessing. Thank you Francis for bringing me home to God. Thank you for bringing me home to everything which is good. May our hearts burn in a great flame so everyone will find the light we find, enjoy the tenderness and strength we know. May everyone celebrate each day as you do, Francis. Despite your pains and trials you celebrate. And I celebrate with you!

Francis I heard that you said the Church elders should smell like the odor of sheep? Is this true? Yes, we are all sheep following our Lord as He protects and takes care of each of us. With His staff, he leads the way. Do you think the Church elders will take off their perfume and live side by side with the people in the streets? Do you think the Church bishops will be common sheep like the rest of us?

Francis, I don't know if you actually said this or it just appeared in my heart. We are all just fools for God!

I will never forget when I found you Francis. You were in the square at San Rufino Church in Assisi. You spoke and my heart leaped. I never thought I would hear such words. I knew in that moment I had found you and that I would follow you wherever the Lord took you. You were in my heart fixed from the beginning.

We are witnessing life's beauty as the path to find God within our-selves, our neighbors, and especially those we turn away from. To put our judgments aside and open our hearts. You taught me this Francis and so much more. There is a love story began long ago. We and every-one are playing our part. We are challenged where do we say "yes" and where do we say "no"? Francis you have risen "yes" in my heart and in the hearts of many.

Today, I sit in my garden. With each Rose is another Rose ready to flower. I am reminded that inside my heart is a peace, next to this peace is a special quiet, and next to the quiet is gratitude. And then there is devo-tion, emptiness which is beautifully full, light, simple being, and on and on. There are worlds and worlds of Heaven within each of us. I remind myself to take the time, be in my garden, and let it bloom for me and all my beautiful sisters to enjoy.

Forever yours,

Clare

Silence:
Letter from Francis to Clare

Dear Clare,

$\mathcal{I}$ have moved on. I am now resting on another mountain peak, breathing the vista of the Rieti Valley stretching out below. Everything is quiet. I hear only stillness outside and within. I rest in holy silence. Sister Wind comes by once in a while and keeps me company. Her gentle chatter is just enough to touch my loneliness. Each day, at least once, sometimes twice, I see Brother Hawk as he swoops down and climbs high above me. He reminds me where to direct my thoughts.

My thoughts are in the silence. There is a great silence within. When the world is not knocking on my door, there is another door. God is on the other side. Slowly this door opens inside and there He is! Every day, every time He is different. Our Lord has a face of silence. Endless silence is His smile. His eyes glow with peace. Such peace it is difficult to look at Him directly. I wait anxiously watching his mouth. It does not move. There is not a word spoken. In the emptiness of the quiet, the silence shapes and forms my mind. I let go of expectation. Why do I expect so much instead of enjoying what is? Silence. I let go of disappointment. Why do I judge myself? Why do I see sin? Silence. When I look in the eyes of my Lord, there is no sin. Yes, there is no sin. Love, only love, a special love dressed in peace is overwhelming present. Why do we spend some much time looking at the darkness in ourselves and each other? We should receive the light. The great silence within is teaching me. God is pure forgiveness. There is nothing else. We are to receive the great light of this forgiveness and sharing with the world!

I have learned something more. Even though my heart is small, so human, once I go inside the silence of my heart, God extends forever. During the night, my bones rattle. The pains in my chest come and go. But I am free, Clare. Freedom is in the silence.

The silence washes my soul. Every part of me is washed. My Lord is washing my hands, my feet, my face. Peace is washing all of me. In the silence, I don't carry anything. I don't carry any thought. I just try to be. There is so much God!

Clare, on the mountain, minutes are hours which pass into days. Words disappear. This world melts away. There is a Heaven, Clare. Yes, there is a great Heaven. I find the silence unveiling a greater silence which can only be described as Heaven.

Yours,
Francis

More Naked than Naked:
Letter from Clare to Francis

Dear Francis,

I feel you drifting off into another realm. A part of me is afraid I cannot follow you. Another part of me is filled with joy. Let go Francis, let Brother Hawk lead you. Don't let me or anything of this world hold you down. You can disappear in the silence. You will not get lost. Our Lord knows you.

May the silence hold your bones until each is still in peace. May the silence love your chest until you breathe freely the infinite. Oh, Francis your journey tears me apart and brings something special inside of me into my heart. It must be love. What else besides love can destroy so much and give so much?

Francis will we still share the little moments, a biscuit, a walk when you return? Will you return? I walk my prayer walk, wondering who is Francis now that the wind and little creatures run away with your mind, leaving your soul naked? Francis, you are now more naked than naked. Meanwhile everyone is buying clothes they don't need, dressing in riches to hide behind, judging everyone by what and how much they wear.

In your nakedness, Francis, I know something is growing that will change the world. I don't know how I know this. I just know. Be the sacred dirt for everyone. Be the simple soil for all of us who are too afraid to be naked, so ordinary, so boldly human. Let Brother Sun and Sister Moon watch over you. Their light is enough. Meanwhile God's might will move mountains inside of you. All your doubts will be pushed into the great seas. I feel this. Somehow I am on the journey with you. Your pilgrimage has taken another path, a path which has no past, no future, only right now.

In my own simple way, I am with you Francis. Yes, I am with you. I don't call you into this world. I no longer call. I am here. I am here Francis. I love you!

Forever Yours,

Clare

The Birth of Our Lord and Meeting with Brother Death: Letter from Francis to Clare

Dear Clare,

After a full moon and a new moon, one morning the sun awakened me in great joy. My body rose and my arms stretched to the sky. Brother Hawk was all excited flying overhead. I knew it was time to move on. So with Brother Leo and dear Brother Masseo we set out for nearby Greccio. Local villagers met us. They were surprised that we come in the heat of the summer. They expected us to return at Christmas to celebrate the anniversary of the appearance of the Christ Child just a short time ago.

We joined them for afternoon coffee and stayed for evening meal. Each villager wanted to recount their experience that Christmas Eve. Each wanted to share exactly what they saw and felt. Their memories were like yesterday which is often the case when God appears in our lives. These memories are something more than memories. When truth appears it doesn't disappear. It stays in the front of our mind and heart forever.

I too enjoy seeing and feeling once again what occurred. It was sunset Christmas Eve. We were gathering some sheep, a donkey, straw. We were waiting in a small barn on the hillside only meters from where we were now dining. We were sitting in expectation of the birth of our Lord. Christmas was coming. Little did we know that that night something would happen that would be much more than another Christmas.

The Christ Child appeared in the straw right in front of us! I went over to pick Him up in all the golden light. The villagers were crying. I was crying. I think the sheep and donkey had tears in their eyes as well. I am told after that night, the making of a simple nativity scene has spread to other villages and towns throughout the region. On Christmas Eve families and friends sit together for the birth that is coming, the Prince of Peace.

I explained to the villagers that I come in the heat of the summer because there is another brother that I am here to meet. There is a brother I want to get to know. They just assumed I was waiting for a brother of ours who was coming in some days to join us. I climbed the hill and went into my little cell at the little monastery on the hill above their farm. I began my meditation, my dialogue with the brother I came here to meet. After a day or two, I don't know how long it was, this new brother came into my cell and joined me. His name is Brother Death. I had been visualizing my dead body in front of me when I looked over and there was Brother Death sitting on the bench across from me. He was smiling as if agreeing it was a good thing that I was looking at my dead body, a good thing to get to know death, a good thing to get to know one another so we would not be strangers.

Most people avoid Brother Death until it is too late. He can come quite suddenly. Meanwhile they have no relationship, no understanding. The fear of Brother Death can be large in the back of the mind. This fear limits our joy. It limits our life song, limiting everything good that is present. I wanted to get to know Brother Death. I thought there was no better place than Greccio where the Christ Child had so clearly appeared to me. Somehow I knew the Christ Child and Brother Death were related. And this day with my dear Brother in my cell with me, I knew he agreed.

Brother Death did not talk but his appearance in my cell said everything. I continued looking at my dead body on the wooden floor in front of me. When I closed my eyes, I had a surprise. I saw the Christ Child. He was inside of me! I would open my eyes and again see my body before me. I would close my eyes and there was the Golden Child. With Brother Death sitting across from me, the clarity of the Christ Child inside became brighter and brighter. This continued for a long time, opening and closing my eyes. The Christ Child inside of me was becoming brighter, brilliant light. As I looked into the light I began seeing the sunrise, the sunset, my brothers, the animals, trees, the planets and the stars. I began seeing life as it really is, magnificent, full of light.

Suddenly I understood. As I make friends with Brother Death, our Lord becomes more alive. Without my fear, the light is brighter! God is so much. Gratitude falls down my cheeks from the bottom of my heart. It's like the sun and moon have come out from behind the clouds for the first time! It's like life is just beginning. There is no reason to fear. Christ is born.

Thank you dear Clare, thank you for your letters. With you in my life, the sun and the moon are dancing the great dance, the dance of beauty, the dance of life! And I am dancing with you.

Yours,

Francis

Understanding Distance and Differences: Letter from Clare to Clare

Dear Clare,

I write a letter to you, a letter to myself. As Francis explores one mountaintop after another and climbs the peaks and valleys of his soul, I am left to explore myself, my small heart and soul here at San Damiano. Is this how I thought the journey was going to unfold? No, of course not. My mind had its own plan. When I ran away from home to follow my Francis, I dreamed of traveling to the ends of this world and entering God's world with him. I thought I would be by his side visiting the remote hillsides of this world and together we would leap into the unknown. Side by side, heart next to heart, we would pour out our heart, our all and everything to our Lord. We would feed the sick and walk with the poor. We would travel together from village to village speaking to the hearts of the forgotten people and letting them know they are not forgotten.

Instead I find myself here, every day, and once in a while a letter arrives, or one of the brothers comes with news. From a distance I hear of the great adventure of my Francis. I hear his news not in person but from a piece of paper or the lips of a brother whom I really don't know. Can this brother actually tell me about the God, the great love, Francis is discovering? Francis is climbing places no pilgrim has explored before. I want to be there with him. I want to meet Brother Death with Francis! Imagine if we held the Christ Child in our arms together!

Instead of Francis and me together picking up the great sword of truth and bringing it to the people, we dream and each make our own journey within. We are alone in the great fight surrendering to the light.

I dreamed it would be me and Francis walking the streets of small and large Italian villages. We would enter Rome together. I would be leading the white horse with Francis riding on his back. Together we would be pronouncing the good news. Instead I am here with my sisters going nowhere. Francis has turned himself inside out meditating on a remote hillside. Where normally it is his personality which shows itself to everyone, Francis is now more naked than naked, his soul is now exposed to the world.

As I grow in spirit, I must admit I suffer sometimes in my heart. Those I care for can be quite distant. Differences in personality can stand out clear and uneasy in front of me. I feel apart. I must admit I also suffer these feelings with you, my dear Francis. I know you are called to the mountaintop, called to far away villages. You must hunt and fish for new brothers to join your order. But when the truth touches my tongue, I must admit I miss your presence, your words, your heart beating here for me and for my sisters.

Forgive me Francis but Sister Wind is airing out my heart today. I must write this letter, even if it is a letter to myself. Do I place this letter in the box under my bed and ask the Lord to carry it as well? As the wind gently blows, today I sit in my garden. My new young sisters from Austria sit with me. They are shy and awkward with our way of silence and prayer. Their hearts are pure and eager but they don't really understand. I know this feeling because it was how I felt when I first ran away to join you and your brothers. What do I do now that I have run away? How do I begin the heart full journey? And now several years later, I feel I am beginning all over again. Every day it is a fresh start. Can I find my Lord in my heart today or do I suffer? Inside I am still a young girl full of hope wanting to find the rainbow with my Lord standing inside. I want so much, perhaps too much. I see these young sisters, I see my mother and sister here who have joined me. We all have the same dream and the same disappointment. Yet we all continue to dream. My sisters and me, we did not make this journey to live with one another. We came together to dream. Each of us is suffering the hope and despair of our dream as we try to get along and live with one another. This family dreaming, we live the best we can with little food, little comfort. Each day I must ask who will wash the laundry? Who will clean the floors?

Francis, I am fortunate. I am still young. I still make my prayer walk every day barefoot over the convent stones. Some of the older sisters feel the body growing weaker, the dream growing stronger with little or no answer.

Francis what is important is not where we are apart but where we stand together. Our Lord is our anchor. No matter how much distance separates us this anchor will always pull our hearts back together. This anchor keeps us still in God no matter how the waves blow in the great sea of life. We are anchored in His love.

After reading, rereading over and over again this letter to Clare from Clare, this letter to myself, I realize I am meeting Brother Death. This is the letter announcing my death, the death of my dream. May it be for me as for you dear Francis that now life begins.

I pray that my Lord forgives me for all my selfishness. I give thanks for my Lord who is perfect love. Francis we are blessed.

Yours,
Clare

Visit to Sister Jacoba, Visit to Rome: Letter from Francis to Clare

My dear Clare,

I have not heard from you in some time. I trust you are well in your little garden of San Damiano, the garden of your sisters, and garden of your heart.

I am in Rome! Sister Jacoba has opened her warm home and to be honest she has opened her kitchen to me. She feeds me hot biscuits and cakes with fresh honey. My brothers ask about my vows. They ask what about holy poverty, chastity, and obedience? I smile. God gives rules for man. Man is not here for the rules. We should not let rules determine our heart but ask the rules to guide our heart to greater love.

Anyway, I tell them I am not visiting Sister Jacoba but Brother Jacoba. She is a great brother and should be respected and be treated as such. When she visits our camp she should be welcomed as a brother and brought to me immediately. I know there is a rule about no women visitors. But as I have said, rules are to support the heart and not the heart to support the rule! Someday Brother Jacoba will make my burial shroud and she must be allowed to dress my body. This shroud is my wedding dress. I will be on my way to Paradise. My Lord and I will be finally coming together for all time, never to be apart.

Brother Jacoba and I discuss the Church and the life in Rome. It is said a local bishop is meeting with the leader of the Jews. Despite the local gossip of unhappy Christians. This makes me happy and hopeful! It seems the bishop and Jewish rabbi are old friends. They often meet and dine as family. They discuss everything. Of course our Lord, his Mother and Father, all his disciples were Jewish. So it should be completely normal for our bishop to dine and enjoy the friendship of this Rabbi. Jews and Christians should dine with each other often. Instead of hunting down non-believers or those who believe differently, we all should be sitting together. Religious leaders need to do more than have dialogue. They should set the example of finding joy in one another's company! We should bring gifts, feast, and dance until the great God in every heart is giving, feasting, and dancing. People of all faiths should break bread and be together in silence. The bread and silence will put our doubting thoughts to rest and lead us to simple peace.

Sister Jacoba and I eat more biscuits and look inside our heart. Jews, Christians with different beliefs, those we call heretics and heathens all have the same heart. Every heart is warm and inside there is Holy Light. The God of all, loves his children.

Dear Clare, I do not know my next steps. For now I enjoy some cake and honey.

Rome is a busy city, so I am certain to return to the forest soon. May you be free in your heart, full of peace, the peace that never lets you down. Be lifted, be holy for all.

Yours,
Francis

The Secret Garden:
Letter from Clare to Francis

Dear Francis,

In the last days I have been spending my hours while the sun is rising and while it is setting in our garden. Seasons are moving fast and I don't want to miss anything. The swallows scream as the sun is rising and they continue their flight song as the sun sets. Soon they will be leaving on their long journey, not to be seen again until next spring.

The garden is full of every color, every smell that ignites the senses. My heart is full as well. I try to convince the sisters to not be in a hurry but come sit with me. There is always something to do. The soul needs our attention. I tell the sisters in the garden we can concentrate. There is the inner garden, the secret garden that the Lord offers in our heart. Perhaps even better than the chapel, it is in the garden surrounded by the flowers of Earth that we can uncover the flowers of Heaven. It is the Roses which always catch my attention. They have no purpose but beauty itself. Maybe they are teaching the purpose of life? The path of receiving the beauty of life!

We must not let our minds wander so much into worry or judgment. We need to concentrate. We need to be resolute and unwavering. There can be so many distractions. The mind can wander easily in some superficial direction of its own. We must sit and be and let the Lord dress us in His beauty. Each of us has to search deep inside for the humility to receive. This love, this peace is not for the weak of heart. We must be mighty and tender, magnificent and vulnerable. Our hands must be empty for the angels to lead us into their secret garden.

It is for this secret garden that we give up so much. It is for this secret garden that we give up the joys of family and the pleasures which most enjoy as normal life. The mystery of the secret garden calls upon all of our heart to give so much. It is a special calling to give up so much and an even more special calling to receive so much.

I am afraid most of my sisters are neither called to give up or receive as much as is called for. Holiness is very demanding in its patience, sweetness, and infinite care. Dear Francis, I have thrown down my dream to find the Lord's dream inside of me. It is a dream of light, a great light. It is a garden, a secret garden that I cannot share because in the words it loses its magic. Yes, it is magic!

I know you too, dear Francis have found this garden that words cannot help but trample even with the most loving attempt. For now, we must help the sisters and brothers by showing them the gateway. This is the best we can do.

So I tell my sisters be not in such a hurry. Sit with me in the garden. Let the beauty all around bring us inside to what the Lord has stored away for us. In the most tender and vulnerable place within the valley of our heart, a secret garden unfolds. The peace will guide us, thrill us, telling us we have given up nothing but been given everything. This peace is where the Prince of Peace sits and waits for us. He is all patience, sweetness, and infinite care. The secret garden Francis continues to grow in the breast of all who have a humble heart. When we can share this garden openly with true love we will know Heaven has come to Earth. Until that time, Francis, our hearts sing in the great silence of the forests, the rivers, the mountains, and the seas.

I think of you and all your little friends. May the grace of the little creatures bring you simple joys on your journey.

Yours,
Clare

Yes, the Creatures:
Letter from Francis to Clare

Dear Clare,

How did you know? I have been spending more and more time with the creatures that fly, those on four legs and even those who crawl along the ground. Recently near Assisi there was a large meeting of birds. Seemingly every kind of bird was present. I asked if I could also attend. They nodded okay. The people think I was talking to the birds. But no Clare, if we want to talk to the creatures we must listen. They will tell us what is in their little hearts if we give them a moment. The creatures have so much to share and give if we have a humble step to receive them. The birds that day grew into a large number because they thought it was funny to find a human who would listen instead of giving orders.

More recently I was visiting some brothers near Gubbio. The people there are scared. The children are frightened because a wolf is attacking the villagers. They asked me to have a word with my brother the wolf. I did not have to walk far before the wolf was in my path. I said to him, "Why do you scare the villagers? Why do you frighten the children?" He informed me. "It is the people who are chasing me." I apologized for everyone. I apologized and Brother Wolf became my friend. We both had a good laugh as he followed me back to town and shared apologies all around. The town's people brought him food and he licked the faces of the children.

I don't understand why we think peace is so difficult. A little humility can heal a lot of fear, anger, a lot of self-importance, which is the root of our conflict.

Shortly after my encounter with the wolf, I was hiking high in the hills where the snow never melts. I was greeted by a bunch of robbers. They wanted my purse even though I had no purse. I offered in all sincerity my robe but they thought I was making fun of them. They were not as easy to talk with as the little creatures. The thieves proceeded to beat my brother body. They threw me off the side of the road into a bank of snow leaving me to freeze in the woods. They didn't like that I was laughing. But I was not laughing at them. I was laughing with God at how seriously we take our demands, how important we think we must have our way, how unimportant is this body when we have a soul and a King who carries us now and forever.

Dear Clare, we cry with the hard minds of men. We cry with joy with every soft heart. We cry. This is the blood of our soul. This is the life. May the flowers of your garden hold you closely and whisper to you all their secrets. I will come visit soon. I promise.

We will share everything!

Yours in our Lord,
Francis

Healing Hands:
Letter from Clare to Francis

Dear Francis,

People are coming. Each Sunday for Morning Prayer the people come from Assisi, Bastia, Perugia as far away as Cortona and Florence. They stay afterward and come forward asking for medicine and a miracle. We share what herbs we can find in the garden. What do I have but my empty hands? With our Lord, however, my hands are not empty. Every broken bone is a call of a broken spirit. Every pain is a cry for our Lord's embrace. The doctors make healing so complicated but love is what really matters.

This Sunday an old lady came who could barely walk. Her arms were deformed, her face swollen. She couldn't talk but her eyes were dancing. I could not help myself. I ran up to her and hugged her and held her and hugged her until every inch of my Lord was now her Lord as well. A giant smile appeared on her face. Her feet straightened out. We walked into the garden and cried together for a long time. It was a good cry. Finally she said, "I am ready now. I am ready to go home." She rose and took my arm and walked beautifully out the gate and down the hill. I know someday I will see her again, we will meet in Heaven.

For each person, I remember they are a soul. It doesn't matter the face of their difficulty. Their soul is beautiful. God gave me hands to heal. I touch their soul and they touch my light which is the breath of my life. I give everything I can and the Lord keeps on giving.

Come soon, Francis, my hands and heart are ready to serve you the herb tea your body needs and the spirit that your heart deserves. Come soon Francis. The olive trees out front are waving in the wind this morning in a big welcome!

Your little sister of the heart,
Clare

The Other Side:
Letter from Francis to Clare

Dear Clare,

Your words are more true than true. We feed those He can feed. We give healing to those He can heal. Through our simple lives, we ask the world armies to stand down and turn their swords into helping hands with food and medicine for many. The Church's bank of gold and silver is sitting in old rooms gathering dust. Meanwhile too many young children want clothes and food to go to school. I know your heart will inspire many to be more interested in giving than having, teaching us how to love instead of wanting to be loved.

But Clare, there is a greater need than healing and feeding the poor and this is to help the poor in all of us. We all are so poor as long as the great divide remains. We all are poorer than poor as long as we are separated from Heaven. Everyone has parents and grandparents, brothers and sisters, and often children, on the other side. Death has separated love ones, separated families and this separation is not necessary. God is here. The other side and this side are together! We are one. We must be our light which does not exclude anyone, especially our loved ones who have left this world but are nevertheless very much with us. We must teach everyone how to heal the great divide, to receive, actually absorb the great light which includes all beings.

Love, Clare, love, this will bring us together. Often in my walks I meet an old farmer who tells me she has lost her husband. Then she proceeds to tell me not long after the funeral he visited her in a dream or he was suddenly standing in the kitchen. He was smiling. He was telling her how happy he is to be in Heaven. "I am waiting for you," he says with his smiling eyes and heart. I don't know how many people have told me these dreams, these stories of loved ones communicating everything is love.

We must talk about this love. We must tell people that these dreams are more than dreams. These visits are not people's imagination. God is real. Our families and loved ones may seem far away to our minds but in our hearts they are alive. Love is here. There is no great divide as long as we light the true flame. It is not a question of belief. It is a question of love. We begin by remembering our loved one and before we know it, the memory is much more. Their presence is with us, living in our heart. Eternal life and this life are one. It is the same with God. It is not a question whether we believe. It is a question of love. Do we love God? Do we enjoy his presence in our heart and our lives? The great divide will end.

The lion will lay down with the sheep. You and me Clare, no matter where we are, no matter how seemingly apart, we are together on the path, going home hand in hand in the brilliant light. Yes, heal with your empty hands and see the angels in your empty heart. Lady Poverty, in all her majesty, shows us the emptiness which is the answer to so many of our questions, so much of our difficulty. Everyone thinks too much and lives with too little heart. The load of their thoughts is the great barrier between them and the angels. The heavy mind keeps people away from the lightness that is the soul in us all. This is why we love Lady Poverty. This is why she talks to us about emptiness. Why does everyone carry so much when the Lord is already carrying us? Our minds are the great barrier to the vast meadows of the heart.

Together, we tell everyone to throw their thoughts into the river and feel the cool water at their feet. God is here. The angels stand with us, wet, surrounded in light. We see them. More important we feel them. Our loved ones and God are all around us.

Yours in the light,
Francis

When the Thoughts Stop and Heart Begins:

Letter from Clare to Francis

Dear Francis,

You are so correct. My family is the aristocracy, the best of Assisi. I had the best private teachers from Rome and Florence. My father has his own private army. But what good is the best education, all our possessions, if we don't have possession of our heart? This is why my mother and sister have joined me in the great run to God. They followed me, following you to sit as a family of sisters in my little garden of San Damiano. In the peace of our garden, the noise of our thoughts stops, and the voice of the angels begins. If people only knew, everyone would run away from all their possessions for the simple company of the angels.

It is not a question of believing in angels. It is a question of having a quiet mind so our hearts can see and witness what is. It is the angels that are the truth. They stand firm in the soil of my garden and yes firm in the garden of my heart. I could describe them. I could paint their faces and try to find a golden color to paint their heart. But Francis you already know them and see everything that I see. This is why our letters are just letters. There is so much more behind the words inside each of us.

People think too much, worry too much instead of being with the overwhelming peace. This simple peace is no further away than the silence. No matter how much silence people have in the fields and hills it does no good if they have no silence of the heart. It is said the abundant God in the quiet. I have heard his divine being unfolded in the weeks and months sitting in the stillness of retreat. May all understand, our King and Queen is found in the emptiness of the silence in our heart.

There is a world of little thought and great heart. This world has no barrier. There is no divide between Earth and Heaven. When the great divide of the mind and heart is healed, love is everywhere. Oh, Francis the sky is so blue today! Do the people see it or are they too busy making plans, doing everything they think must be done? I stopped my sisters this morning and told them to come, to look. Maybe some of them thought I was mad. I told them the sky is calling us. One sister looked at me. She was in a hurry to make the noonday meal. I insisted to her please stop. The endless blue sky is the sky of our soul. If we take a minute and drink this sky with all our heart we will be so full there will be no need for a noonday meal. Nearby was our pregnant sister. She looked into the sky as if she had found the heart of the child within her. She is soon leaving with the brother to start a new family. This is all a gift from the infinite sky. The endless blue is so much. It is enough!

Francis, today I am in love. Expectations and disappointments of not too long ago have vanished. I do not know where. This is the gift of a giving Lord. There is so much God. Francis you are part of this big God for me. I shall see you soon. Be well as best you can. The body is the altar of God for now, so take care of your poor body. Someday we will drop this body for our Heavenly body but this is another day. Today there is blue sky. Dear Francis, there is only God, so much God.

Yours of the heart,

Clare

The Church is Dead:
Letter from Francis to Clare

Dear Clare,

I dreamed last night the Church is dead. Inside every chapel is a simple tombstone where it is written: The Church Died in the Year of Our Lord 1221. Nothing more, nothing less, the Church is dead. In the dream I was surprisingly feeling okay. Now what? The building was completely empty. The priests and people had gone home. The doctrine, the rules, were no longer. The pews were gone. As I looked at the altar it opened, and there was a big sky, a big blue sky. Immediately, I thought, "God is alive! Life is everywhere! The Lord is alive!" I walked outside the Church and the sky was full of light!

Then today your letter arrived about the blue sky. In this moment, I understand the dream.

Why do we spend so much time and effort maintaining old buildings? Why do we argue about rules and doctrine when we can be in the light of the blue sky? Why do we listen to so many words when we can be directly in the heart of life? I remember now as I tell you my dream that in the blue sky, in the light, was the form of something I can only describe as an angel. In the brightest part of the sky, I am sure there was this love which I can only say was our Lord, Jesus Christ.

If we find joy, the church will rebuild itself. Instead of worrying about how to rebuild an old Church full of scandal and rules which every normal person says make no sense. We should empty ourselves and let the pure joy within wash the old into the new. Yesterday is gone. Tomorrow doesn't exist. Today is all we have to feel the joy.

Our Lord did not ask for a Church stuffed with old rules, hoarding money collected from the poor, defending itself against all those with complaints. In fact, it was because of the Temple of his time he came and announced God is here. He preached under the blue sky! He went freely wherever He was invited, and touched whomever welcomed Him.

Today I'm telling my brothers to embrace the blue sky. Some look at me as if I have gone mad. But others laugh while closing their eyes. I know they have found the infinite joy, the new church rising in their hearts.

Clare, I think my dream was a gift from Brother Death. He is teaching me. Why hold on to what is of the past? Why spend my life being busy with the dead when joy cries out? Why try to organize an order of brothers when I could be in the garden with the beauty of the growing flowers?

Thank you, Clare, as always, thank you for your light!

Yours,

Francis

Little Flowers:
Letter from Clare to Frances

Dear Francis,

My sisters have been so busy lately that I had to finally tell them to stop! We don't want to be busy Martha when our Lord is present and here for us. Francis, He is here! The silence in the chapel is so thick, the peace can't be anything else but our Lord. Lately this special quiet has spread into the refectory and the dormitory. During the evening meal the other night there was so great a presence that everyone suddenly stopped eating and just sat. More than one sister had tears rolling down their cheeks. My sisters are not normally ones who get emotional with these sort of things. Some of the sisters report to me that they cannot sleep at night. They don't want to miss a single moment of being with our Lord. I understand. When the stars are this bright, the soul is completely awake to each moment of the night. The soul and the Divine dance in times like this.

Anyway today, even though the sisters want everything prepared before Sunday guests, I asked them to stop and sit with me in the garden. The little flowers are breathing a sunshine of perfect love. I tell the sisters that the little flowers are our teachers. They give their all in their short time with us. They give their color, their perfume. They hold nothing back. We too must offer everything! Then in the simplicity of our heart, the love is suddenly everywhere!

I explain to the sisters that in their offering, they become free. Hold nothing back. Offer and rest in the Holy stillness you find waiting inside.

I confess to them this is not always easy. I offer my loneliness. Sometimes I begin by offering my doubts about my heart, my path. Am I worthy of the Divine which comes and settles in my emptiness? Am I fooling myself with the feelings that seem to rise out of the nowhere within? Is this really God or my wish for something special? How do I know? So many questions, so many thoughts. I offer these. I offer my human self which finds no end to small complaints, worries, and desires. I offer my thoughts about how everything should be and how it actually is. These thoughts cannot help but look into the mirror of my own heart. There is no saint living here. Just poor Clare. I explain to the sisters we are poor not because we lack anything but because ultimately we are not in control. It is our Lord's mercy which frees us from so much self. It is our Lord's love which allows us to be so close with Him. I remind them that we should not be too busy offering all of the self which sticks to our soul and forget to receive the sunshine, the love. I feel this is our Lord's wish. We are not to be so busy with our self that we forget to enjoy his companionship. After all this is why we were called to be sisters, His sister!

The sisters seem to appreciate hearing my journey, my trials, the twists and turns to find my heart. You would think it was miles, somewhere far away. It is right here but so protective and hidden. Why do I hide from God? He knows every hair, every thought even before I think it. We each are so human and so hungry for the Lord's promised meal. Is it fair that some of us find the banquet while others try and try the best they can and find little reward for their efforts? Of course they hear the story about doubting Thomas and how blessed is he who believes who has not seen. But I don't want my sisters to just believe, I want them to see and enjoy what I see! I try not to judge or question but is it fair that we share the same Lord, the same garden, the same life and some suffer while others dance in the Lord's company? We eat the same Divine Bread. We drink the same Holy Wine.

Sometimes dear Francis there are more questions than answers. Then I come back to my garden and be with the little flowers. They seem to have solved all these problems. I am just going to give my all the best I can and let the perfect sunshine have me as it wishes. I love being a bride of Christ. He makes me infinitely happy today. The love today is even more special because my sisters stopped to enjoy the garden silence with me. We were all bathed in a great outpouring of love! Yes, Francis today in a perfectly clear sky it was raining love. We were all soaked, wet, sitting, going nowhere. Even the two sisters who normally seek but do not find, they got poured upon! There were big smiles on their faces. We were all together in the garden with just one wish in our minds and hearts. May this love soak every part of us!

Francis, can you feel it? Let's pray that all who seek that they too will find. May they be wet, very wet in our Lord!

Your,

Clare

Our Leper Friends, the Little Flowers: Letter from Francis to Clare

Dear Clare,

Yes, the path of the little flowers is our path. We want to give our heart to the beauty that is not seen. We want to appreciate life in its simplicity, in the joy of the moment. When our friends, the lepers, give simple thanks after we wash their sores, pour water over their hands and feet, their small thank you is enough. It is more precious than anything one can find at my father's large clothing store, the bakery, or any other gift this world has to offer. Our leper friends are leading us on the path of true joy, the joy of finding life's real rewards. Each one of them is an innocent child, our Lord in disguise. This is our path Clare, to find our Lord in his many disguises, to love the innocent children, all of them!

Yesterday a big storm blew into our camp. Many of the brothers were wet and cold. The evening fires had not had a chance to be started so everyone was wet and cold through the night. I thought of my leper friends. They too are wet and cold probably with no fire. I thought of the town's people up the hill behind the stone walls of their homes, safely warm for the night. There are many thoughts during moments like these. Have I chosen the better life? Maybe I am fooling myself and misleading my brothers? Surely God doesn't love us more or less because we have a fire or nothing for the night. I am no better or worse than the souls down the road living as lepers. I am not so different than everyone living up the hill behind their stone walls. We all have the same wishes to be warm and fed this night. How much of our path is pride and how much is real? How do we really know if we have found the better way? So many thoughts. They find no home. I let go and just be with the stars breathing above and sister wind stroking the trees to sing. I let go and find myself dressed in a world of complete beauty. Then I remember why I chose this path. I chose to live in the greater beauty of life instead of worrying about how to stay warm and how much do we have to eat. I chose to marry the stars and sister wind instead of worry, desire, and thoughts which never find a home. Life is my home, Clare. Yes, life is my home and every moment of beauty is a little flower come to rest in my heart. Our path is to give our hearts fully to the little flowers of life. This is enough. May everything beautiful and everything ugly have a home in my heart. Who am I to judge? Welcome one and all. Welcome!

Your,
Francis

The Garden Is Always Perfect Just As It Is: Letter from Clare to Frances

Dear Francis,

Thank you for your letter. I don't think being cold and hungry brings us any closer to God. But I do think if we are not preoccupied with being warm and full, we are hopefully more available for God. I too question our path knowing the more I look into my heart, the more I see the heart of all. I don't want to think we are special because we have our Lord's presence as our intention. Our intention can quite easily be infiltrated with pride and self-importance. Who is to say our Lord's presence is more Holy within our convent walls than the family walls of the people in Assisi? Who is to say our errors and laziness to love where love is needed is really that different from our neighbors? When we really look at ourselves truthfully, we are as naked and human as anyone else.

This is where our doubts can begin to flood the purity of our heart. This is why we must keep our Lord's presence in our mind and our heart. Yes, we are human, but our cup is empty for Him. This is the difference. Most people their cup is for whatever they find in the moment without regard to eternity and the bright light of Heaven. It is the brilliant light bursting in my heart that tells me to stay with the path. I try to keep my concentration and to let the silence be my keeper. There are so many voices in the world. But the little voice of the silence is the voice which lifts our hearts into our true destiny!

Francis, in my breast the bird of Heaven sings. I cannot describe her song but its melody is soft grace for every pain and every question. I am sure you hear her too. This is the brother sister way we have given ourselves to. This is the marriage of Heaven and Earth which carries us in storm and sunshine, when hungry or full. The moon has her phases but she is always the moon. The sun has her moods but she is constant in our hearts. Tonight I listen to my little bird singing. This is my soul reaching out to you Francis, reaching out to all beings, reaching out. And this is my Lord picking us all up in His embrace. Wherever you are in this moment Francis we dance in His embrace!

Truly yours,
Clare

My Heart, My Promise, My God: Letter from Francis to Clare

Dear Clare,

If I am going to say Yes to God I must say Yes to life. I must love everything, everyone. My God, my heart, my life are all the same.

I know each man is no better or worse. Dressed in fine jewelry or cleaning the floor, we are all Divine souls in human clothing. I know those who are certain they shall be first will probably be last. And those who are last will undoubtedly be first. It is the difference between holding a position of power or a position of service. It is the difference between defending the faith or practicing the faith, between wanting to be right or wanting to love. Every day, every encounter is simple bread full of the presence of our Lord.

Your, Francis

Simple Bread, Our Little Miracle: Letter from Clare to Francis

Dear Francis,

Your words, simple bread, my hands tremble. I don't want to cry in front of the sisters but tears roll down my cheeks all day after reading these few words. I know they come from the deepest cave of your heart. Yes, so much is given, so much is present. I have this feeling when I am totally present with this bread, the stars grow brighter, the trees stand taller, all the animals have laughter in their gait.

I must share something more with you. Don't tell a single soul. I am sure you, only you will understand. Speaking of bread, recently this has been happening quite often. A neighboring farmer suddenly appears with fresh bread for us. He seems to arrive on the very days when our cupboards are quite bare. Somehow he knows just when we are getting hungry. But the moment we sit down and begin to eat this bread, I swear to you Francis, it is not bread! It is the actual love of our Lord. There are no words. Our bodies, hearts, and souls are overtaken! There is a presence which can only be described as love more pure then pure. I just sit there in awe and of course, tears. Many of the sisters have the same experience. The others cannot help but feel the peace that is suddenly in the room. We don't tell anyone. But I can share this with you,

Francis. Maybe this is why my tears could not stop after reading your last letter.

Thank you dear Francis. Thank you that I can share so completely!

Your,

Clare

More Thank You Then I Can Say:
Letter from Clare to Francis

Dear Francis,

Today I find myself reflecting on all the good which has come into my heart, my very soul, since we have met. The Church was alive the moment you entered my life and it continues to breathe fire and water in my soul every time we meet again. You are the pilgrim's pilgrim on the way to Heaven. Every day I sit at the empty table in my heart, sit waiting for my Lord. When you are here, Francis, we sit at the table together! It is such grace that I have you in my heart sitting with me. The Lord always comes, but when I am with you. He comes with a whole banquet!

Yes, your visits are a banquet for me and my sisters. Thank you for sharing your heart including your grief and your joy. It all is part of the Divine Journey. Your footprints are so naked and true. They help me and all the sisters to find our way. There is so little truth in this world. We appreciate you as an example. Your humanness opens the gate. The Divine swings down with your vulnerability, your laughter, your tears, with the big God you have uncovered. Thanks for letting us see!

Francis, I always feel the perfume of your soul in my heart but when you are here I feel your goldenness in my hands and my feet! My whole body is awakened. I say yes again to the choice we made to follow this path. My whole body soaks in the truth of your body so wounded in illness yet so beautiful in its human glory. Know my Francis, I pray for your physical pains every day. Surely God can show his love beside the rocky path he has given you. I do my best to pick up these stones for you in my prayer and throw them aside so you can have a moment of rest. You deserve a path not of stone but smooth sand as you walk into the great ocean.

Francis, when you bless us with your company, I find a great victory inside. Where normally in my meditation I sit with the emptiness, the light, and the vastness, my mind often leaves the wonder and thinks about my sisters. I worry too much. I think too much about what we are going to eat. I worry is it too cold or too hot? Will my sisters be able to sleep tonight? I know my sisters are not my children but it seems the Lord has given them to me as children to hold and care for every day!

Francis, when you are here I can go much deeper within. My thoughts stop. The Divine really begins. Your journey is so true that it washes away my worldly self. In these times, I too can be where you are in the great adventure! Every day, I explore the valleys of my heart, but when you are here the colors are more vivid, the love more exquisite, the peace is beyond the peace this world can offer. Yes, there is also sometimes the great nothing that you know so well sitting in the arms of Lady Poverty. But to be clear, when you are here the nothing of nothing does not come forward in my heart. Only you Francis, only love is here! With your presence nearby there is not a single part of me that is left alone. Maybe this is why I can fully be with my Lord.

I go inside into this place which is difficult to describe. But I want to try to find the words, Francis. I love having someone to share it all with. There is another world very far away, totally different than the world around us. I feel my soul going away or maybe it is coming closer? I am in a space surrounded by thousands of stars in the distance. The air is intense yet extremely gentle. My being is absorbed in the greater being which is all around me, in me. My body is gone. There is only awe, this air of love. I don't know where I am but I trust. It all is in my heart. The heart is the home our Lord gives us to get to know Him. Trust is no problem.

This space, this realm is without thought and feeling. There is only my breath. Very slowly I breathe and experience it all the best I can. It seems every time I visit this place I am finding more of my real self. I am coming home. Slowly, this unlimited being I find within is becoming more of the self I share with my sisters and the visitors who come for healing. I worry less. I am more full of God. This place beyond anything I know in this world is yet mysteriously a part of our world. How would I otherwise be able to visit?

Oh, Francis someday I will go into the deepest ocean of my heart never to leave it again!

This is my prayer, the reason for every step I take. When I talk with a sister, gather herbs in my garden, when I drink my tea, when I sleep, and the moment I wake up, my heart leaps to join Him! Every day there is no other reason to exist but to find Him and this love which is beyond love, His peace which is more than peace.

Francis when you visit life is more alive. Thank you from the bottom of my heart.

All the sisters have a lighter gait today. Their toes are dancing! Be well in your travels. We travel with you!

Your sister and friend,

Clare

I Step Down:
Letter from Francis to Clare

Dear Clare,

How beautiful! Your words, your heart. You are opening the gifts which only those who can see will see. Yes, the gifts are even more beautiful when we open them together. Grace! Glory! And Peace!

The people don't understand our love. The Church does not understand real love. This love is not about suffering. She is not about being poor. Love is this vastness you talk about. She is this peace beyond peace. She is the body when we let go of concerns about our body. This is why I go from one mountaintop to the next. Love is calling me. The view of the valleys below helps me to sit inside in the expansiveness without end. So much God!

Clare, thank you, your prayer for Brother Body. I am sure each word is heard. The longing, purity, sincerity of heart is what prayer is all about. Meanwhile brother body is not old but weak. Our Lord gives me lots of illness, yet I am given a world beyond body, beyond words, a world of infinite quietude. Every day we live in God's body so the trials of Brother Body are not so important.

Now I am again at Fonte Colombo. Not long ago I had this nightmare of the doctors visiting, wanting to heal my eyes. They thought the best medicine for the infection that would not go away was to use a burning red-hot iron on me. Yes, they heated in a strong fire the branding iron for my eyes. I prayed to brother fire to have mercy and prayed hard. By the time I was finished with my prayer, I told the doctors I was ready. They could proceed. But they told me the operation was already completed! You see, Clare, the Lord carries me over the worst of my ailments including the medicine my brothers find to try to help me.

I wonder if my Lord will carry me now. Dear Brother Elias is asking me to give a new rule for the order. He wants me to think of the needs of the organization. He says the brothers want a program, meetings. They want a plan for the future. I tell him, "How can you plan for God?" But he says I should either take responsibility for all the brothers gathering or resign! Resign? Resign from what? Resign from my Lord?

I am afraid we speak different languages. Elias speaks of rules and organization. I can only speak of the love and peace you describe. The words on his tongue are foreign to me. I prefer not to speak at all. If I do speak it is only if I am blessed to find some words by the grace of God. I am never sure what if anything He will leave for me in my heart. Brother Elias asks me to step down. I think he is right. I'll step down if this means I can step into the arms of life and everything that is given. When the brothers talk about organization I remember my dream of the death of the Church. With the talk of organization, I see a cemetery. Maybe this is not fair but this is what I see, graves everywhere.

Speaking of graves, since I am no longer in charge of the brothers, I can travel. My heart yearns to be in Jerusalem! My brothers say it is too dangerous. But I am not afraid.

I am going to Jerusalem. I will write again soon.

Your brother in all worlds of love and joy,

Francis

Jerusalem!:
Letter from Clare to Francis

Dear Francis,

I know you know that Jerusalem is surrounded by armies. The Muslims are chopping off the heads of Christian soldiers including the children they brought along for the Crusades.

The Christians are chopping off the arms and legs of the Muslims. I do not know who is winning, as if there are any winners in such a world! And my Francis yearns for Jerusalem!

My body says "No!" but my heart says "Yes, you must go!" Where else in the world is our Lord most needed but in the center of this Hell on Earth, Holy Jerusalem. When you arrive hold me in your prayer. Tell our Lord to have mercy for they all do not know what they are doing! I will try to get some brothers to bring you some honey and a sweater for your travels. Your soul will determine the journey. Where I would close my eyes to all the blood and gore, you will see only Christ wherever you are taken. Carry the true sword of your heart proudly. No-one, no army will stand between you and your destiny.

The seas can be rough and the boat of this life fragile but you will be victorious. I can feel it! Francis, it is said Jerusalem is a golden city with temples everywhere full of wonder. But I think when they talk as such they are talking about another Jerusalem, the one they will find after their heads have been removed from this Earth! If it is God's will, you will keep your head because your soul and heart are greater. This world still needs you.

Travel well. Travel with me in your breast. Travel with miles of God all around you in every direction. When you meet the Muslims I know you will embrace them. Embrace them for me as well.

Your sister in eternity,

Clare

The Good Fight: Letter from Francis to Clare

Dear Clare,

I think of you and our time together, as I wait for a boat to carry me toward the Red Sea and beyond to Holy Jerusalem. I am with you in your inner garden today as always. Your garden oasis is a gift without end. I don't know what the future holds but the paradise of our heart is true today and, God willing, tomorrow.

As I wait on the dock for a boat to carry me into the unknown, I can't help but think of all the blood that has been poured upon the Earth, blood of both Muslims and Christians. We all are part of this history of so much blood, so little love whether we were on the battle fields or not. I try to be the humble servant asking the world's armies to put down the sword. What can I or any of us do with such an inheritance? What can one man, standing in sandals, hope to accomplish? Even if I wear no shoes like many of our poor, do you think they will understand? Do you think they will realize the war, all war is over?

The days pass and there is still no word when a boat is coming for me. I spend my time also thinking about my talk with brother Elias. I fear for my brothers. Clare, we started this march of the heart, from the heart to the heart of God, to be free! We are free of organization, free of programs and plans. We called every brother and sister to come and celebrate the good life with all the flowers, animals, rivers, mountains, planets, and stars. And now I am asked to step down so an organization can be built? I am traveling to the Holy Land, leaving my brothers in the land of meetings, discussion, everything but the joys of being naked before God?

Sure there are brothers Leo, Masseo, old Sylvestor, brother Philip, and others. There are many brothers who will not go to meetings but sit by the river and listen to the moving water, the current of their lives. There are brothers Moricus, Giles, and hopefully, brother Peter from France, who will climb trees, feed the birds, and help the farmers plant their crops. I am left thinking about all the others. Brother Catani is with Elias wanting to lead in another way. Are my brothers now to be busy with discussion about what, when, where to find Holiness? It's as if the mind knows the answer for these questions. How can they discuss the future of the Order when they know there is no future, no past, only the grace of God's presence moment by moment? This is why we gave up our worldly life to be with the simple peace. It is the simple peace which controls my fear and desire as I wait on the dock for my journey.

Waiting is never easy to me. I think patience on the spiritual journey is the most difficult task. I am ready, yet I must wait for the boat of life to take me on to what I don't know, my calling.

Clare, be soft and happy in your garden. Be soft and happy for all of us. As the world fights its battle against the heart, you fight the good fight. I pray you will silence your thoughts to nothing less than the gentle sweetness of our Lord!

Your,

Francis

No Use Trying to Control What Only God Can Control: Letter from Clare to Francis

Dear Francis,

There is no waiting. The simple peace is with you in every moment. I try to tell myself this as I and the sisters wait news of your journey. Are you on the ocean headed for the Holy Land? Are the ocean waves too large, too rough? Is Brother Body very hot in the ocean sun? I worry you don't have food or fresh water. Have the Muslims found you? Do they hold you captive? The mind can so quickly escape the simple peace when it wants to. Why, Francis, why do we run from the peace, the quiet? Why do we run from God when He is so present, so giving?

Finally my soul understands, I have no control over what I have no control over. My mind at this point falls back, gently into my heart. The great room opens inside of me. I am absorbing my Lord and my Lord is absorbing me. I am dissolving into God and God is dissolving into me. The I and me and we and Thee lose all boundary. I am home.

When I find the vastness of my heart, I know this is the home of my soul. What do I do now? Do I pray to be an instrument? Maybe I should not be busy and just sit still? The vastness has no beginning, no ending. Who am I to think I have some purpose other than just to be with and in our God? Who am I?

Francis today I simply am, nothing more, nothing less, lots of nothing. There is love in this nothing. Life is a beautiful carpet of love and nothing woven together. I am sitting before my Lord, in my Lord. Dare I say, sitting on this golden carpet, I am the Lord?

Excuse me, I must stop writing. The convent bell is ringing. Church officials all dressed with official documents are at the front door. They say they come representing the Bureau of Official Doctrine. I show them around. They enjoy that the convent is clean. They want to know what we are doing? Exactly what are our hours of chapel and what do we pray? I tell them we suffer for our Lord. In the chapel the sisters sing for the Lord. They seem to want to hear these things. I want to tell them that we don't suffer so much. We don't sing so much. We mostly just sit and be with our King in his Holy Chamber, the chamber of our heart. But I can tell they don't really want to hear this. They wouldn't understand. So I stick with the suffering and singing. They seem pleased and after only minutes are ready to move on. They stamp something official and leave it with me. They declare, "God bless Mother Church," make a sign of the Cross, get on their horses, which are also dressed official, and depart.

This is the life today in Church and the home of my heart.

Be holy Francis for the whole world. Be holy! Surely, you will find everything sacred!

Yours,

Clare

Finally the Holy Land: Letter from Francis to Clare

Dear Clare,

ays turn into weeks, no captain wants to risk his head to take me to the Holy Land.

Finally I stole away, hiding on a small boat bound for North Africa. All your fears came true. It was so terribly hot I thought I would fall overboard into the ocean. I was hiding in the boat so I did suffer from little food and no fresh water. The Muslims found me but not before I had a walk through the battlefield. I walked through all the lines, Christian and Muslim. Dear Clare, don't be so critical of your fears, your thoughts. Maybe your concerns were whispers to God to remember little Francis? He watched over me! I am afraid to ask what fears you have now that maybe I should know about. Clare, in your humble spirit, you and the Lord are one.

You are right about so many things of Heaven and Earth. The ground everywhere I looked had turned red. There are body parts everywhere. Our Lord is present. I don't think he sees Muslim legs and Christian arms. He is standing in the middle of the battlefield. Many angels are in his company. They go around and pick up the souls of the fallen. I don't see them separating the men by religious belief. They are bringing them all together into this garden. There is a bright garden of light surrounding the Lord. The Lord has bathed all the fallen in this brilliant light. The soldiers are stumbling in shock. They are in horror of what they have just done to one another and to themselves. The angels are touching, lifting every soldier from the ground. Each soldier is slowly waking up as if he had forgotten about God and all the love. Many of them have fallen before the Lord asking, "What have I done?" They are looking around, back and forth. Their eyes are now filled with light. They are asking again and again, "What have I done?"

It's a good question for all of us! I continue walking through the Christian line and then the Muslim front line. The Muslims are standing, surrounding me, staring as if I am mad. I carry nothing. I tell them I want to see their Sultan. I tell them I want to see the great al-Kamil. They seem pleased that I know his name and show proper respect. They take me to him. After a small test of faith where I offer to stand in the fire along with his priests, the Sultan smiles and gives me a gift of a beautiful prayer horn. I am free to walk anywhere, through all the lines of his army. I am free to walk to the Holy Land!

Clare, I am on my way to the Holy Land! The sun is shining and Holy Jerusalem is just ahead.

Your,
Francis

The Saracens Are Here!
Letter from Clare to Francis

Dear Francis,

You were supposed to be the one throwing your body at the mercy of the Lord to visit the Holy Land. I was just going to sit here in my garden, safely at San Damiano. The Saracens are here! Yes, the Muslim army is camped just below my convent. The sisters are terrified! I have instructed them to go into the Chapel and pull the latch to lock the door. Each of them is to be perfectly quiet. I tell them they are now sheep. Under their breath they are to think only this, "The Lord is my Shepard!" with all their soul and all their might, they are to hold on to the Lord. He is our good Shepard!

I go out front to stand between the army and my ladies. They are marching right toward us on the way to the walls of Assisi. I stand with my Lord in my breast. I am holding the monstrance, holding the Body of Christ high in the air above me and the approaching army. They see me. I am standing boldly with only the Lord, the King of Kings in my hands and my heart. The army stops and stares at me. I am staring only at Heaven and my God. There is only God in this moment! The Saracen army proceeds and goes around our little convent. We are safe. We are in the Lord! Yes, there is only God!

To be honest, my heart missed many beats. Our pregnant sister had to be carried to her room. She is soon due. Her man, husband soon to be, is making preparations. They are already talking about the beginning of a lay group of Franciscans. They want to start a small group of house-holders who want to follow in your footsteps. Yes, they can be followers of Francis, and be free! The Lord calls all of us, each in our own way!

After the army passed our convent walls, many of the sisters cried. We have a generous God. Our prayers have made a shelter for us and for many. Everyone is safe. Our garden of little flowers is safe. The holy love we know continues.

Now we wait word from you Francis. Tell us about Jerusalem. Send us word about the Holy Land.

Your sister with humble heart,

Clare

Jerusalem:
Letter from Francis to Clare

Dear Clare,

    After walking through the desert like the Holy Family from Egypt to the Promised Land, I found myself in Jerusalem. There is not a Christian in sight. Me in my simple robe and my prayer horn, as gift, are allowed to enter. I eat the same figs and nuts our Lord once tasted. Jerusalem is the city where Christ has risen. It is said the Muslim God Mohammed ascended to Heaven from here as well. This should be the friendliest city in the world, welcoming all. A great spirit of love and truth should be in every street and corner. Pilgrims of all religions should own Jerusalem as sacred ground. Here the whole world should come together to embrace and celebrate everything that is good.

    I'm ashamed to say I find no sacred ground. The soldiers are drunk. The people are frightened. Many poor and ill fill the streets. There is no charity. I find no love. It doesn't matter which army is here. It is the same. Do they really think they can own God with the sword and spear? Poverty and illness rule the people. Riches and power attract the soldiers. Christ and I am sure their Mohammed, are nowhere to be found.

    Shortly, I come home. What can one soldier of love do to stop so much hate, arrogance, and mistrust? I could plant my feet in the old city center and pray and scream out. Maybe some soldier would come over to me and cut off my head for making a disturbance.

I am coming home. I am coming back to you, Clare, my brothers, and my sisters. I am coming home. I return with a broken spirit. I should know better than to expect God to be in history and stone when He is in my heart. I risked my head and converted no-one. The armies are still at each other's throats. The poor are still poor. Can you blame the unbelievers when armies for God behave the way they do? I can only blame myself. My crusade is over. I return home and ask our Lord for forgiveness. Maybe when no boat arrived for all those weeks to bring me here, it was a message! Clare, I seek God's forgiveness for me and for all the madness that occupies this part of the world.

I am alone. My brothers are being organized at home. The Church is fighting wars not of love but of blood. I am alone. Is there a friend of the soul, a friend of joy anywhere?

Am I the only fool for God that wants to swim with the fish, fly with the birds, and crawl with the little creatures of the Earth? I am alone. All I see and hear is "no." I ask for just one simple "yes." There is no heart. I am alone. Clare, I am coming home.

I offer a drink of water to a beggar on the road and even he doesn't find a smile. God has disappeared from here where everything should be so much God. I don't blame Him. The armies patrol. The people hide in alleyways. I am free to travel as I wish and the only place to go is home. Home is the company of one believer. Home is the company of joy. Soon, Clare, I leave these waters for the water that quenches thirst. Tonight there is a new moon. Sister moon gives me hope. I hope she pulls our boat quickly out of these waters into a safe harbor, a harbor for the soul. I am tired. Brother body is sore. Maybe my heart rests tonight. Tomorrow is a new day.

Your friend,
Francis

Rescued by the Sister Dolphin: Letter from Francis to Clare

Dear Clare,

I don't know if you will receive my last letter. Maybe it is lost. It was written in a time I was lost. But now I am found. A boat came quickly to pick me up to carry me back to Italy. Sister Moon each evening is slowly growing and my spirit is also returning. The sea is like a vast glass bowl, very smooth, very lovely and delicate. Each day dolphins are swimming behind our boat. They swim right alongside the boat, leaping, singing, welcoming us on the Divine journey. This morning we stopped and anchored. Two shipmates and I dove in and swam with the dolphins. They came very close, probably to see if I could float! My soul feels rescued, freed by Sister Dolphin.

Word has arrived from my brothers. Somehow they knew how to find me. Brothers Leo and Masseo will meet me when we dock, when we reach land in Ancona. They say a wealthy baron in Bologna wants to become a brother. He wants to be free of all his possessions including a mountain! He wants to give the mountain to me and the brothers. I accept this mountain as the last place I will climb in my reach for Heaven.

Clare a new day is coming. I can feel it. For myself, I have learned a lot. In the great river of the heart I cannot push and pull on the river as if it should bend to my own desires. I must trust more and listen to the heartbeat of the river of life. I must dive deep. Swim to the shore as I wish. Most of all I must learn to let the gentle stream carry me. Yes, our Lord carries us. This is the only way into and through His gate.

Clare, I am carried! I am well. My spirit grows in the joy of sister dolphin leaping out of the glass sea. I give great thanks for all of God's creatures. They remind me we are free!

Your brother,

Francis

Yes, the Hearts of Everyone: Letter from Clare to Francis

Dear Francis,

I rejoice in your safety from the dark winds blowing so strong. And I suffer with you about the brother trying to organize God as if love is something we can make on our own.

Francis, we dream and hope for a new Church but do we really think it is possible? Can the Church of riches and power become the simple stable of Lady Poverty where our Lord was born? If we live the simple life and find a little God, I don't know how it can change the much bigger Church? All we can do is love God and find God in the poor, the poor in spirit of everyone. We lean on God and learn of God from our Lady, Lady Poverty. She walks with us each step of the day. She sleeps next to us at night and is there first thing every morning. Lady Poverty empties the room, clears the mind, opens the heart for our Lord to be present each moment of each day. This is the path we offer. May it glow in the dark for those who want to come.

In our vulnerability, we discover trust. Trust is faith that is in the heart! Lady Poverty teaches us to live a life of great heart. Here is a well of God, a well of great being. In this well we discover the sacred waters of patience, simplicity, and generosity. In this well we discover the light! Without Lady Poverty we would not know of this light! We hear stories.

We read the Gospel. But without Lady Poverty how would we know our heart? I am in love today with Lady Poverty! May this love carry you, Francis, and me, into eternity!

Your,

Clare

Yes, Lady Poverty and Sister Chastity!: Letter from Francis to Clare

Dear Clare,

Lady Poverty is everything you say and so much more. She is the door. Through Her, we find the realms of God inside of us. Everyone has their way, their certainty how God is and how He should be worshiped. Lady Poverty reminds us that the true religion is beyond our thoughts and judgments. Most people think about God. Lady Poverty tells us about vulnerability, to receive the love. She reminds us not to be preoccupied with this world so we can discover the world of something much greater. There is so much more to life than worrying about managing the affairs of home and business and worrying about what everyone else is doing. She empties us so there can be a home for God inside of us. Lady Poverty takes my hand and leads me into my heart to God's glory. She is never far away. When I am sad, when I am full of song, Lady Poverty is with me. She is my best friend, the friend of every pilgrim. She is hiking alongside of me in every step.

Do you think the Church can understand that Lady Poverty is not really about this world? She is the simplicity so we can be in the golden world within. She dissolves our minds until there is only a great vastness, the Heavens, the planets and stars, the world of eternity. I know you know Clare this place of the heart where there is no thought, only unlimited being. Lady Poverty sits with us in this place so we can continue to explore and discover the true lightness of being. She smiles as we smile in all of God's presence!

It is here in the heart that Lady Poverty introduces us to sister Chastity. This pure place of the heart is the home of our dear sister. I remember the time I threw myself in the thorny arms of Sister Rosebush. I didn't know what to do with all my feelings about my sexuality, my loneliness. Sister Chastity was standing by me, laughing, jumping up and down, trying to say, "No!" She said, "How can you say no to life and yes to God? Why do you think Brother Body is worth less love than all the creatures you adore and appreciate?" I realized that after all the years, I had punished Brother Body as if this is a way to discover love. I must worry less about sin and sing more of love! How will the people find Sister Chastity unless they embrace the heart? We are all human with desires and fears. Nevertheless, Sister Chastity, is here ready to take our hand in the whiteness of our being, the peace, the pure, wordless Divine inside. She is our friend. She is not judging but dancing. She is in joy every time she finds someone to dance with. In her laughter, we see a glimpse of God inside of us.

Clare, as the brothers debate policy and doctrine, I am trying to end all debate and rest in the heart of my heart. This is enough. My body hurts but I, me, who I know myself to be, is very well.

Yours,

Francis

Our Mother:
Letter from Clare to Francis

Dear Francis,

Today, after our walk, we returned to our monastic garden. With flowers all around us, we sat in our circle. Brother silence was strong. In the center of our circle, one of our sisters brought out an Icon brought to us from France. Our Lady, the Holy Mother is pictured smiling. She is pure, accepting everything, giving everything, the perfect Mother. We sat with her a long time.

Lady Poverty was sitting with us as she always is in moments like this. One of my sisters remarked that she comes from an educated family where she was taught not to worship paint on canvas and board. She was only taught about the God of reason. She shared how our Lady Poverty has taught her the limits to thinking. The sister, with a tear in her eye, told us about finding her God of love. Her words were milk and honey. "Our Mother holds me when I am not sure what to think. She holds me when I am angry and when I am afraid. She gives me my heart. She brings me to myself, Holy and whole."

Another sister spoke up. "In our house, we had the same God of reason. My family ignored the poor, ill, the need of those who lived next door. Without the God of love everyone in our house was lonely. They were more poor than our poor neighbors.

Agnes, my sister asked us to please forgive her. She realized how controlling she has been in the kitchen. She apologized for telling us what to prepare and how to organize the kitchen. "Lady Poverty," she shared, "is teaching me to give up being so controlling. I try…" All the sisters began to laugh. "Lady Poverty," I said, "is asking all of us to give up control. She wants to take us into the inner garden."

Francis, it was a beautiful peace in the garden. Every sister gave thanks for Lady Poverty showing us it is much better to be naked with our Lord instead of trying to be in control of the kitchen, the chapel, or cleaning the convent floors!

I imagine you have reached land by now. I pray you are now walking arm in arm with your brothers. Maybe you are already in Bologna, or climbing your next mountain?

Joy for you, Francis, only joy, perfect joy…

Your,

Clare

Perfect Joy:
Letter from Francis to Clare

Dear Clare,

Yes perfect joy! Perfect joy is risking my head to get to the Holy Land only to find blood and body parts everywhere. Perfect joy is to meet lots of drunks, unbelievers, and beggars who don't even want a sip of my water! Perfect joy is waiting for weeks for such a voyage. Perfect joy is finally coming home in the company of Sister Dolphins and landing in the arms of my brothers, Leo and Masseo. God is great! God is joy when all else says "No." He is here saying silently, "Yes! Perfect Joy!"

Yes, we are climbing the next mountain. This mountain is not the same as the ones before. This time I understand perfect joy! I am climbing and with each step I am giving our Lord everything, the pain, and the beauty. I am giving Him my all and everything. La Verna was given to me. Imagine, my Lord wants me to have an entire mountain!

I don't know how long the climb or our stay will be. Somehow I think Francis is climbing up the large hill but it will not be Francis coming down again. I don't know how to say it but the separation from my Lord even though it really is quite small, must end! Yes, even a little distance is too much. My soul cannot bear to be alone for another minute, no less another day! I must, I have to be united with My King, My Queen, the Kingdom. If there is only God, how could it be otherwise?

Early this morning, I was on our hillside with brother Leo sitting nearby when I looked over at him and he appeared as all light. He was giving so much light. Then I noticed the tree behind him was also light. Each branch, every leaf was shimmering, giving light. Then I saw the rocks around us were light. They were not solid but moving light. The little insects, the birds walking about, were each dancing light. The hut where we slep last night is light. The chair, my cup, each are gifts, offering, giving such bright light.

Our Lord is literally in everyone and everything. Even brother body, all my aches and pains are made of light! Clare, I don't ask how I became so separate from this light? I am what I am. The journey has been what it is. The light humbles me. All the light washes me of me. We live in a world of endless light. In truth there is only our Lord in all His many forms of light.

So Clare, I write to say goodbye. And I write to say hello as if for the first time. I write not to be dramatic but to ask for your prayer. I don't know. I really don't know what is going to happen. Do I pray for mercy or no mercy? Do I pray for blood or for glory? When I no longer exist who is praying and for what? Lord, only my God, and Lord, I am a lover too often without my true love. This is ending. Something new is beginning. I can feel it with each step as we climb. Clare, I am climbing, climbing!

Blessings, Clare, nothing but grace and blessings for you and your sisters,

Always,
Francis

My Cry and Scream of Pain & Delight!
Letter from Clare to Francis

Dear Francis,

It has been some weeks and maybe longer since your last letter arrived. Last night I was sound asleep and then suddenly in the middle of the night I awakened. I screamed! I could not help myself, I screamed, "My Lord! Where is my Francis?" In that moment I knew you were gone. I could no longer find you in my heart. There was no Francis. But there was more of my Lord. Francis you were gone and you were more present than ever.

I couldn't help but scream and scream. My mother and sister came rushing in to hold me.

I cried Francis. I miss you and I know you are more with me, more now than ever. I miss you and I know you and my Lord have united!

Are you still in your body or has my Lord completely taken you? Are you still with us on this Earth or have you been taken completely? My mother and sisters held me in their arms. I was lying in your arms, Francis, for a long time. Many visions came to my mind and my heart. I saw a giant seraph flying overhead, flying above you as you lay in the woods. He had a spear which he penetrated your body with. I saw blood coming out of your side, your hands, and your feet. My God, Francis you are now one with my crucified Lord! You are now the crucified one! What has happened to you?

I could feel His pain and His bliss has penetrated your body. You have been forever branded. Body is now soul and soul is body. You Francis and my God are One! Yes, I cry and I scream but it is not for sorrow Francis. I know now your climb has been completed. The climb is over! Yes, after all the mountaintops, you have climbed the final mountain.

I am with you, Francis. Perhaps I am with you now more than ever.

Your poor sister, rich in your soul as always,

Clare

Letter to Your Donkey: Letter from Clare to Francis

My dear Francis,

I hear you have come down from the mountain. You and our Lord have come down together. You carry His wounds and He carries your soul. The brothers tell me your eyes are on fire with a Heavenly light. They tell me your body is slowly bleeding from your hands, your feet, and your side. Brother Donkey carries you from village to village for believers and non-believers to see with their own eyes. Please Brother Donkey go safely, smoothly, my friend and Lord is now on your back.

I believe Francis. I believe you have been given the ultimate gift. You deserve this and more. My sisters and I are at your feet. We are with your heart and your poor body. We hold you tightly in our prayer. Your love has become love's body. The pain and the bliss are one as it must be. Francis there is no other way for you. All is how it must be! You and the Lord had to unite in this way. And Brother Donkey will carry you for as long as we have the grace to have your company. I imagine you are now more God than Francis. Your poor body, I am told, is now carried in the thin arms of only Lady Poverty.

These are Holy times. Yes, holy times. It must be for this reason God has found you and never let you go. He was with you on the entire journey and then he decided nothing else is left but to carry you the rest of the way. This is a great time for you Francis but it is even a greater time for all of us. Everyone must celebrate. God is so present, here, for all to see. Heaven and Earth, heart and mind, love and more love have come together!

Your sister on Earth and in Heaven,

Clare

Dreams:
Letter from Clare to Francis

Dear Francis,

Days slip into weeks which slip further into months and months. I do not hear from you but we are more together than ever. Where before my heart was shared with you and my Lord, now you are inside my Lord and He is fully in you. You and He are one in my whole body and soul. I am happy knowing that you are riding Brother Donkey traveling through the countryside spreading the Good News to everyone. Francis, I know you are home inside. The humanness and the Divine, the pain and the bliss are no longer at odds, one battling the other. Peace, true peace has come. They say you radiate light out of your heart and of course your wounds. Sometimes I do wish I was with you to wash and bandage your wounds. But you are being carried in greater arms than I could provide.

I am writing you to tell you about more of my dreams. I understand you no longer receive my letters but I also know you know and feel me now more than ever. So I write and cry and laugh. Francis you are free and so am I!

Now the dream! You are standing alone in a small stream. The light of Brother Sun is dancing upon the water. The little birds are singing nearby in the branches. You are well. You are in nature with your friends, cooling your wounded feet and hands in the water.

Suddenly a horse comes galloping through the woods. There is a brother dressed in a white tunic approaching. The rider gets off his horse and walks toward you. It is then that I can see who it is. This rider is our Lord! The King of Kings is climbing down to the river to be with you, Francis. There are no words being said. You both seem to know one another!

Our Lord leaves his sandals on the shore and joins you in the river. The light of Brother Sun is now dancing around both of you, shimmering on top of the water. Our Lord takes some water in His hands and reaches above you and blesses you. He takes more water and it pours over your heart. You kneel down in the water, lift one foot and then the other, and kiss them. Our Lord is standing there with a big smile on his face. Peace, an otherworldly peace surrounds you both. Light is glowing, yes shimmering, brilliant.

The light from Brother Sun or from God, it is not clear where it is all coming from, but it is getting much brighter. A very bright light is around you, both are dancing, streaming seemingly everywhere.

You are happy. You embrace our Lord, He holds you for a long time. You walk together a short way down the river and then He goes back to his horse and is gone. In the silence He rides away and you remain in the water. There is nothing but light.

The peace of this dream stays with me. May it stay with me forever. Then just yesterday, Francis, I had another dream. In this dream you appear to me with all your love and all your heart. I start to share my dream of you meeting our Lord. You raise your fingers to your mouth as if there is no need to speak. You're smiling. You already know, "Yes, it's all true." Without words you continue, saying, "It's all true. Everything is true. Soon it will be only God and Heaven for me and for you. We leave Mother Earth and join Father Heaven as both join and melt into the hearts of everyone."

Thank you, Francis, thank you!
Clare

Afterward

After the death of my friend and spiritual brother Gerardo, I sat with the letters of Francis and Clare for a long time trying to understand all that was being said, all that was happening. During this time we moved from California to Assisi and would end up living in Assisi for twelve years. There is so much to learn and appreciate when the hearts of Francis and Clare are so close!

During this time we discovered right underneath the apartment where we were living was an abandoned large room. It was the courthouse in the time of Francis and now in ruins needing reconstruction from the earthquakes. We thought how perfect to restore the courthouse in Assisi, now making it into a chapel with altars of all religions for pilgrims to come and sit together in the peace of Francis and Clare. Pope John Paul was coming to Assisi with the world's religious leaders and our chapel would be ready for anyone who wanted to come. The Pope even sent us a letter complementing us on our efforts and sending the local Bishop to give a blessing.

But what about the letters?

Dear brother Gerardo didn't understand that I am yes an author, but not well known. I have no connections really to give out The Letters. So the magic of Francis and Clare just sat in my living room for some years. In the year 2012, we left our retreat center in Assisi with a team of friends to continue to offer retreats for pilgrims looking to find the journey of Francis and Clare within themselves. We returned to California to begin a silent retreat center near San Francisco. During this time, the new Pope

Francis was coming into office. I thought how exciting! Francis is here again!

I tried the public waters for the letters, reaching out and publishing a couple of letters in the Huffington Post on the internet. I wondered in the modern era is there much interest in the heart overflowing in love, the hearts of St. Francis and St.Clare? Is there hunger today for the simple peace found in the great silence?

Finally with the publishing of The Love Letters of St. Fancis and St. Clare, I have no doubt as their love soaked souls reached out so profoundly to one another, today they are inviting all of us on the journey of unlimited wonder.

For current information about Bruce Davis please visit:
Retreats in the footsteps of St. Francis and St. Clare in Assisi, Italy
www.Assisiretreats.org
Silent Meditation Retreats near Napa, California
http://www.SilentStay.com